*"You are magnificent."*

*Nella did not know what to do. The major was looking at her in a way that made her feel decidedly odd. Something was happening to her, and she did not understand it. Her heart had begun to thump.*

*She looked up at him uncertainly. No one, Harcourt thought confusedly, had the right to have a mouth like that. Warm and generous and soft, it invited—no, commanded kissing.*

*Suddenly a scream shattered the silence.*

*"What in God's name was that?" the major exclaimed.*

Also by Rebecca Ward
*Published by Fawcett Books:*

FAIR FORTUNE
LORD LONGSHANKS
LADY IN SILVER

# CINDERELLA'S STEPMOTHER

Rebecca Ward

FAWCETT CREST • NEW YORK

Mark Wartski, who saved my computer
and the day.

A Fawcett Crest Book
Published by Ballantine Books


Library of Congress Catalog Card Number: 91-91821

ISBN 0-449-21915-1

Manufactured in the United States of America

First Edition: June 1991

# Chapter One

"WHAT A SUMPTUOUS tea," marveled Lady Angelica Linden. "Are we expecting guests?"

Her elder stepdaughter, engaged in clearing the tea table of a riding crop, several copies of the *Horseman's Gazette*, and a pen-and-ink study of a black stallion, shook her head.

Lady Angelica clasped white hands in the lap of her twice-turned blue muslin gown and gazed wonderingly at currant buns, toast that was actually buttered, and a rum cake. "Is it someone's birthday, Nella?" she hazarded.

"The tea will fortify us." Miss Citronella Linden's tone was deceptively brisk as she added, "Thank you, Stubbs, and please tell Mrs. Brunce that the cake smells heavenly. Rosa will—but where *is* Rosa?"

"I believe she has gone sketching, ma'am." The ancient butler's wheeze conveyed disapproval. "Miss Rosemary set out shortly after luncheon and was last seen entering the woods."

"She will be hungry by now." Nella's faded gray riding dress swished about her ankles as she walked to the window, threw it open, and leaned out to give a piercing whistle. Angelica started, and Stubbs so far forgot himself as to wince, but Nella said calmly, "I collect that Rosemary will appear immediately. Please do pour, Angel."

Lady Angelica waited until Stubbs had tottered out of the Blue Room. She then asked, "*Why* must we fortify ourselves, Nella?"

Nella regarded her stepmother with affection. She had been thunderstruck when her late father, Sir Thomas, had announced his intention to marry a lady three years younger than his elder daughter, but her doubts had disappeared when she met Angelica. The daughter of an impoverished country squire, Angelica was an exquisite, gentle creature with golden hair, amethyst eyes, and a smile that was both sweet and eager to please.

"Our tea is something like a council of war, Angel," Nella said.

"Sir Tom's debts," his widow murmured. "Are we in trouble, then?"

In spite of herself, Nella sighed.

"I had thought we could manage if we economized, but apparently we cannot. More and more of Sir Tom's notes are coming due, and if we do not take stern measures, we will be forced to sell everything we own."

"Everything?" Angelica paled at her stepdaughter's nod. "Linden House, do you mean—and Excalibur, too?"

An anguished look filled Nella's sea-green eyes, but once again she nodded. "Excalibur, too," she repeated.

Just then the door to the Blue Room was flung

open and Rosemary Linden came marching in. She had a sketchbook tucked under her arm, pencils and brushes protruded from the pocket of her walking dress, and her boots were muddy. When she saw the tea she exclaimed, "Oh, famous! Did anyone die?"

"Of course not," Angelica exclaimed, shocked. "Why would you say such a thing?"

Tossing aside her sketchbook, Rosemary advanced on the tea table. "The last time there was a funeral in the village, the vicar's wife sent us leftover cake and shortbread. 'The funeral baked meats,' and all that." She cut a large slice of rum cake as she added, "What was that you were saying about your horse, Nella?"

There was, Nella thought, no use wrapping plain facts in clean linen. "Excalibur will have to be sold along with everything else we own," she said bluntly, "to pay Sir Tom's debts."

Stricken, Rosemary looked up from her half-eaten cake. "Is there nothing we can do?"

Nella caught hold of her sister's high chair back to stop the treacherous shake in her hands. "One of us must marry."

"Aha," Rosemary exclaimed wisely. "You have had an offer."

She continued to eat cake, and Nella wondered how anyone could be so naive. At eighteen, Rosemary Linden cared nothing for convention or polite society and was happiest when she was tramping through the woods with her sketchbook. She had no doubt been sitting on some mossy spot today, for there were grass stains on her dress and a wisp of lichen clung to one frayed cuff. The face she turned up to her sister was a study in browns: brown hair, a sprinkling of freckles, and ingenuous brown eyes that were as guileless as a baby's.

"Did you have an offer to be married?" Rosemary repeated. "I did not know you had a suitor."

As she spoke, the ormolu clock on the mantel began to chime. The cheerful, tinny sound seemed to echo in the near-empty room. Most of the furniture had long since been sold, as had the Venetian crystal, silver candlesticks, and a Sevres figurine of a lovely lady with dark hair and laughing eyes that had shared the mantelpiece with the ormolu clock. Sir Tom had bought this figurine for his first wife some years before her death.

Nella had cherished that figurine. She hoped fervently that whoever had bought it had given it a loving home.

She drew herself up to her full five feet and spoke dryly, as though discussing the merits of a horse she was about to buy. "No, Rosa, I have not had an offer, and I am not likely to get one. I am twenty-four and so am considered old-cattish on the Marriage Mart. I am also very short—Sir Tim used to say I was too puny to be any good except on horseback. My hair is dark brown, which is unfashionable just now, as are my green eyes. In short, I would not *take*."

Angelica protested, "You are too hard on yourself, Nella. You are beautiful and brave and loyal, and any gentleman who married you would be fortunate."

Nella flashed her stepmother a warm smile but said frankly, "I feel that I am handicapped in knowing too much about gentlemen. Collect that I went often with Sir Tom to Newmarket—he was plump of pocket in *those* days and Ableman was our jockey—and have had a chance to observe sportsmen. They were almost constantly foxed and usually foolish. Indeed, I can tell you that I did not admire them—nor did they admire me."

"That is because you can ride better than they can," Rosemary pointed out. Suddenly, a stricken look filled her eyes. "But . . . but Nella, you *cannot* mean that I must be married. I would dislike it above all things!"

As though soothing a restive horse, Nella patted her sister's shoulder. "Don't be alarmed. You are too young."

Relieved, Rosemary fortified herself with more cake. Angelica faltered, "Surely, you cannot mean *me*?"

"You are the only one with a chance, Angel."

Angelica's teacup rattled in its saucer. "Not again," she cried.

She looked pleadingly at her stepdaughter, and Nella recalled the torments that Angelica had suffered at the hands of her ruthless family. Having no assets except their daughter, they had tried to sell her to the highest bidder on the Marriage Mart.

"If it had not been for good, kind Sir Tom," Angelica quavered, "I would have had to marry Lord Waxe—who was eighty-three and had the gout—or that horrid Mr. Rickdon with his creeping ways and his leer. Ugh!"

Nella ran to her stepmother and put an arm about

her trembling shoulders. "You would never have to marry someone like that," she cried. "We would not let you."

Rosemary reached for her sketchbook, tore out a sheet of paper, and with a few bold strokes sketched a young man on horseback. "A handsome duke will take one look at you, adore you, and heap his riches at your feet," she predicted. "And look—here you are in the lap of luxury, Angel. Would it not be famous to lie in bed all day and have servants bring you sugarplums and coffee and strawberries with pounds of cream?"

Nella couldn't help admiring Rosemary's deft little sketch of Angelica surrounded by fawning servants. "What nonsense you talk," she smiled.

Angelica shook her head sadly and said, "It is I who am talking nonsense. Of course I must marry, and quickly, too. There is no other way."

Nella felt a dull ache in her heart that she suppressed instantly as Angelica continued, "But how can we afford to attract a wealthy suitor? Even with your giving riding lessons, Nella, and after all our economies, we have no money. We cannot even pay the servants who have not left us. Mrs. Brunce and Stubbs and Torfy have not complained, but I wince whenever I think of how much we owe them. We cannot possibly afford a Season in London."

"We will not need to go to London," Nella said.

"But how else can I meet—"

"We will not need to go to London because we have been invited to Lady Portwick's ball."

Nella drew a stiff square of paper out of the pocket of her dress and handed it to Angelica, who cried, "I cannot credit it. Lady Portwick has made it plain that she thinks us below her notice. Her family has descended from a real saint, or so she says, and she considered Sir Tom a godless man. Since his death, she has ignored us."

Lady Portwick was not alone, Nella thought wryly. Since Sir Thomas Linden's death in a hunting accident a year ago, the Linden ladies had been largely ignored, except by his creditors.

She said, "I suspect that her ladyship's secretary included us by mistake. It does not matter. What *does* matter is that Lady Portwick's younger brother, the Earl of Deering, will be at the ball. Where Deering goes, his rich London friends will follow." Nella drew a deep breath and added, "Lady Portwick's ball will be full of men. Wealthy, titled men!"

"You make it sound like a declaration of war," Angelica sighed.

Nella thought of her coal-black stallion in the paddock. She looked toward the nearly bare mantle and remembered the fate of her precious Sevres figurine. She clenched her small hands.

"It *is* war."

"War," declared the young Earl of Deering, "was simpler. 'Pon my word, it was. You was shot at. You shot back. Can't shoot these curst bills, Court."

He swept the back of a beringed hand across the top of his Louis XV desk. Bills, letters requesting payment, and scraps of paper affixed with the earl's signature fluttered down to the fine Aubusson carpet.

Major Charles Harcourt leaned back in his cane-backed chair and stretched out long, booted legs. He clasped his hands behind his unfashionably cropped dark head and surveyed his aristocratic friend with ironic, gray eyes. "Why not just pay them?"

"With what? Bloodsuckers have bled me as dry as a turnip. B'dad, Court, I'm played out."

"You mean you've played the fool."

There was no sympathy in Harcourt's voice, and the earl swore bitterly. He began to pace up and down the morning room of his London town house as the major continued, "In the past month you've smashed up four curricles, lost a fortune at White's and another at Brooke's, and then had to pay for those damages that you incurred at Vauxhall. You can dance if it pleases you, my dear fellow, but don't whine about paying the fiddler."

"To the devil with you," the earl cried. "You know why I've been kicking up my heels. My heart's broke."

The angry flush had faded from Deering's fair, handsome face, and he looked far younger than his twenty-five years. Young enough, thought Harcourt grimly, to mistake infatuation for love.

He disguised the concern in his voice with banter, "Don't talk slum. You heart's been broken fifty times this past year. It seems to have great powers of recovery."

"Hadn't met Lady Barbara then." The earl stopped his pacing and leaned against a window that overlooked fashionable St. James Square. "Court," he went on. "If you hadn't saved m'life, I'd never have met *her*. B'dad, I've wondered since why you bothered."

Rising to his full six feet, Harcourt strode across the room and grasped his friend's shoulder.

"Lady Barbara Hinchin's husband is the best shot in London," he said sternly. "Have you ever thought that she may enjoy pitting him against young fools? Ronald Kierby was her lover, too . . . and he lay at death's door for months with Lord Hinchin's bullet under his ribs." He gave the shoulder he held a rough shake. "There's blood on Lady Barbara's dainty hands."

"How dare you?" Deering shouted.

He glared at the major, who said, "She's not worth going to the devil for, Edward."

Steadfast gray eyes met the earl's furious gaze, and after a moment, Deering gave a gusty sigh. "Feel as though I *am* going to the devil," he whispered. "When I think of Barbara, there's a fever in my blood. I love her, Court. Love her till the day I die."

An odd look, part pain, part distaste, passed across Harcourt's strong-featured face. His fine mouth tightened, and the set of his square chin became harder. "Let me hear that tune in a month," he retorted, "and I'll believe it."

"You don't know how it feels to burn as I do. Doubt

if you have a heart to break, give you my word," the earl exclaimed. "I suppose you'll tell me next that you'll never marry."

"I've no desire to be legshackled in the near future," Harcourt replied cooly. "When that day comes, I intend to marry with my head, not my heart. Which means, my friend, that I'll marry for money and not for love."

"Love!" The earl sank into a chair and put his face in his hands. Harcourt watched him, thinking that Lady Barbara Hinchin with her flaming red hair and her laughing black eyes had driven her poison deep. If he stayed in London, Deering would be drawn back to her flame, and there would certainly be a duel.

The thought made Harcourt frown, but he only said, "These Cheltenham tragedies become boring, Deering. What you need to lighten that Friday face of yours is a change of scene. Why not go down to Hampshire for a sennight, as your sister wishes?"

The earl looked up at this. "Must be weak in your upper works," he exclaimed. "M'sister's the last one I want to see now. Should have been a bishop, Maria should. Gives sermons. Proses on about a fellow's sins. Takes it too seriously that we've descended from that plaguey saint—"

"Saint Hugh the Brave," Harcourt interjected, "who rode in the Second Crusade, converted the Saracens, and became a monk."

"The very one. Must have been a rum touch, Court, to leave his lady and his brats and go wandering off to sing psalms in some monastery. Always seemed to me that he showed a lack of proper feeling to abandon his family, give you my word."

Harcourt interposed, "I used to live in Hampshire as a lad, did I tell you?"

"You ain't told me a lot about yourself, Court. All I know is that your parents are dead and that you ain't on good terms with your relatives. I can understand that, give you my word. Think of m'sister. Besides, if I go down to Hampshire, I'll be far from Barbara." The fleeting interest that had lit his eyes faded away into dullness. "I couldn't bear being away from her, Court. Have to stay in London."

The major strode to the window and flung it open so that a damp fog—redolent with the odor of mud, refuse, and smoke—drifted into the room.

"Hampshire air is clean," he said. "There's good riding down there and pretty country girls. And hunting. Think of riding to hounds, Deering."

Underneath the town house window, a jarvey had begun to curse his horse. The animal's frantic whinnies mingled with a nearby dog's barks and the jarvey's drink-roughened oaths.

"Oh, shut the window," Deering shouted. "I take your point. But to go to m'sister's—b'dad, Court, you don't know her. In ten minutes, she'll have me on the rack."

"Not if I'm with you," Harcourt said. "We'd ride and hunt and fish. I recall some fine trout fishing I did there as a lad."

The earl stared hard at his friend. "You'd come to Hampshire with me? That's handsome of you, Court. But you won't like Maria, I promise you, and

Portwick drinks like a fish. Disguised most of the time, give you my word. And m'nephew's one of those mush-mouthed, chitty-faced halflings that puts you off your feed. Why *would* you want to go to Hampshire, anyway?"

To save your foolish young life, Harcourt thought.

He shut the window and stood looking out into the London darkness for a long moment. Then, turning, he smiled at his friend.

"Why would I want to go to Hampshire?" he repeated. "To relive fond memories, of course."

But his smile did not quite reach his eyes.

# Chapter Two

"Tea, Deering?"

The young earl eyed with distaste the delicate porcelain cup which his sister held out. "Good God, Maria, no."

"I must request, Deering, that you do not use profanity in this house. It does not serve as an example to the servants. Besides, your nephew is a youth of untried years and should not be subject to evil influences."

Deering glanced at the heir to Portwick Hall, who was staring dreamily at a bowl of flowers. "That swill will rust m'inner works," he protested.

"Tea is excellent for your digestion, which, naturally, has suffered from your ramshackle and dissipated ways." Catching the look that her brother shot at the tall man who stood by the fireplace, Lady Portwick added repressively, "I collect that you do not agree, Major Harcourt."

"Ma'am, I bow to your knowledge on the subject."

Smiling, Harcourt set down his own Sevres teacup. Lady Portwick might send him sharp looks, but he had her slightly off-balance, for she did not know what to make of his two-edged comments.

Harcourt continued to smile at her while wondering at the difference between Deering and his sister. Though they both shared the fair hair and blue eyes that had come down to them from their mother, they did not look like siblings. Deering was of medium height, slender, and well-favored with fine, almost delicate features. Lady Portwick was tall, amply fleshed, and had inherited her father's heavy features and small, mean mouth.

Their characters differed, too. Deering, though bubble headed when it came to women, was kindhearted to a fault. Once, he had outraged his fashionable friends by stopping his curricle en route to Vauxhall so that he could rescue a dog that had been injured by a passing carriage. He had wrapped the hurt cur in his new coat, received that very day from Scott, and had taken the animal home so that he could tend it with his own hands.

Harcourt had seen and heard enough of Lady Portwick to know that there was little chance of her stopping her carriage for a dying child, let alone a chance-met mongrel.

And he had *volunteered* to come to Hampshire with Deering. For the hundredth time since coming to dreary Portwick Hall, Harcourt wondered if insanity ran in his family.

There were footsteps in the corridor outside the Green Saloon, and Lord Portwick came in. With markedly unsteady steps he progressed to a high-backed chair, gave it a prod with one thick finger, collapsed into it, and saluted the assembled company.

"Hello, illo, illo," he giggled. "Dashed fine afternoon."

Calmly, his wife picked up a Sevres cup and filled it to the brim. "You will feel much better when you drink this, Portwick."

Lord Portwick scowled. He rubbed his nose until it shone like a beacon of light in an otherwise uninspired landscape. Eyes, red rimmed and watery, surveyed the tea tray with loathing. "I don't want any dashed tea," he announced. "Take it away."

From across the room, Deering grinned at his friend. "A guinea says that he don't take the tea," he mouthed.

The great drama of the day was about to unfold. Would or would not Lord Portwick drink his tea? Would he defy his wife? Not bloody likely, Harcourt thought.

Lady Portwick's eyes narrowed ominously. In compelling tones, she declaimed, "My lord, drink the tea."

Lord Deering looked disgusted as his brother-in-law meekly swallowed the hated beverage. "I was looking for you, Portwick," the lady continued. "Have you forgot that you were to ride with Lionel?"

"Didn't forget," Lord Portwick protested. "Couldn't find the dashed brat anywhere."

"Where were you, my son?"

She had to repeat the question twice before Lionel looked up dreamily and murmured, "I beg your pardon, Mama. The light is so fine, and the chiaroscuro is excellent, isn't it?"

"Lionel!" Even Harcourt started at Lady Portwick's tone. "Leave off rainbow chasing, I beg. Why did you forget to ride with your father this afternoon? You were to meet with Mr. Wickers, the land agent." Then, closing her eyes, she added mournfully, "How you try a mother's patience. A future baronet *must* not forget his appointments."

"No, Mama."

"I collect that you are neglecting your studies, as well. Pray go to your room and spend some time with your books."

"Yes, Mama."

Lionel rose with such haste that he upset his chair. In an effort to right it, he stumbled over a settee at his feet and knocked it into the table that held the tea tray.

"Watch where you are going, my son," his mother admonished coldly. "A future baronet should not shamble about like a stable hand."

Harcourt had had enough. Setting down his tea cup, he, too, got to his feet. "I beg you will excuse me," he said. "My groom tells me that Lancer is favoring a foot, and I must see to him at once."

Without waiting for a response he strode swiftly across the hallway, down the carpeted, circular stairs to the ground floor, and out the door. "Good God," he muttered. "What a family."

It was a relief to be in the fresh air again. Harcourt walked briskly to the stable where he dismissed his groom and saddled his bay stallion personally. A few moments later, he was seated on Lancer and trotting away from Portwick House.

It was mild for this time of year, and the sun was

bright in the blue sky. Harcourt brushed aside a faint sense of guilt at having left Deering alone with the Portwicks—the earl was, after all, related to them—and drew in deep breaths of early March air. There were primroses under the hedges, and the violets would be stirring beneath the soil. A meadowlark trilled its joyful song, and cheerful sparrows hopped about the side of the road. For the first time since he had arrived in Hampshire, Harcourt felt his spirits lift.

As he cantered along the road that led away from Portwick Hall, he caught a glimpse of Lionel's canary-colored coat among the trees. So the lad had *some* gumption, after all, and was probably making for a secret hideaway where he could be free from his mother's tongue and his parents' brangling. "The more things change," Harcourt murmured to himself, "the more they remain the same."

Shrugging his broad shoulders as though ridding himself of a distasteful thought, he spurred his stallion forward. Lancer's powerful muscles made short work of the miles, and soon horse and rider were progressing through broad green meadows bordered by cultivated farms and orchards. It was good hunting country, with high hillocks and valleys that would give great sport, and Harcourt rode appreciatively until he came to the main road. As he turned Lancer to seek open country again, he saw a cart rattling over a nearby hill.

It was driven by a woman. Harcourt had no way of knowing whether she was old or young, for most of her was concealed by a dark cloak, and her face was shaded by a deep-brimmed bonnet. Apparently she had come from the nearby town, for the cart was laden down with sacks and provisions.

A farmer's lass on her way home from market, Harcourt noted casually. Then he saw the curricle come racing over the crest of the hill.

Driven by a young buck in a fashionable riding coat, the curricle was traveling at great speed down the narrow, steep road. Though he was too far away to be heard, Harcourt shouted a warning. "You damned idiot—look out!"

There was no way that cart and curricle could avoid each other. In a second, they would collide. With an oath, Harcourt set spurs to Lancer and galloped toward the scene of impending disaster. But miraculously there was no collision, for the driver of the cart managed to turn off the road in the nick of time, and the curricle passed it and sped away.

Either the farmer's lass was lucky, or she was a whipster of some skill. Harcourt trotted Lancer back down the road, calling, "Are you all right?"

Nella heard him through a sea of dust. She tasted the grit of dust. It was in her eyes, her nostrils. Her bonnet had fallen off, and she had lost her whip somewhere. Her heart was beating wildly. If she hadn't managed to turn old Rumtum at the last minute—

Assuming that the deep voice belonged to the driver of the curricle, she called, "I am unhurt. And your roans?"

Harcourt was astonished. In spite of the rusty black cloak she wore, her manner and her speech proclaimed her a lady. "The reckless fool who drove the curricle does not deserve decent horses," he exclaimed. "If you had not turned as you did, you would have collided."

Nella blinked through the clearing dust and saw a gentleman mounted on a powerful bay stallion. He wore no hat, and his short hair glinted like burnished coal in the afternoon sun. Gray eyes surveyed her keenly out of a hard-planed, strong-boned face. "Are you sure you aren't hurt?" he asked.

She shook her head, but Harcourt noted that she had lost one of her gloves and that the small, bare hand was shaking. He said abruptly, "I should ride after him and give him the hiding he deserves."

Nella shook her head. "Perhaps he had just acquired his roans and he wanted to see how fast they could go. It was sheep-brained of him, but he meant no harm. They *were* beautiful animals, were they not?"

The wistfulness in Nella's voice made Harcourt look at her more closely. The dust had cleared, now, and he could see that she was quite pretty in an unconventional way. Her eyes were large, more green than hazel, and slightly tilted at the corners. Her mouth was unfashionably wide, and her small, straight nose was lightly dusted with freckles. Long, dark hair had escaped from its confining bonnet and curled about an oval face that looked very young.

Instinctively, he gentled his voice. "Major Charles Harcourt, ma'am, at your service," he said. "How may I help you?"

"I am Nella Linden," she replied, "and I thank you

for your concern. If you could possibly find my whip . . ."

It was lying, together with her glove, in the dust beside her cart. As Harcourt dismounted and bent to retrieve it, he noted that the cart's right wheel had come to rest in a deep rut.

"I'm afraid you'll have to get down, Miss Linden," he said, and explained why.

Nella looked grave. "I *knew* I felt a bad jolt as we went off the road." She took Harcourt's proffered hand, dismounted, and stood beside him to survey the damage. "That is a chasm, not a rut," she exclaimed.

She was a very small lady, Harcourt realized. Her head barely came to his shoulder. "The axle must be ruined," she was continuing.

"Let me look." A minute later, on his knees, Harcourt said, "It seems sound enough."

"Perhaps it only *appears* sound."

She had knelt down beside him in the dust, and at such close quarters, Harcourt realized that a light flower scent emanated from her. "Are you sure?" she asked.

"Yes, certain," he reassured her. "I've seen a great many broken axles in my time."

"On the Peninsula." It was a statement, not a question. "I collect that you must be a military gentleman," she went on earnestly, "because the bronze of your skin comes from a hotter sun than can be found in England, and because of the way you hold yourself."

Not only could this small lady drive, her thoughts

were clear and logical. Harcourt listened with growing interest as she continued, "And also, I saw how you and your stallion are in great sympathy. Sir Tom told me that warriors and their horses are close comrades."

He nodded. "Lancer and I have been through a great many campaigns together. Sometimes I think he can read my mind."

Her green eyes lit up. "I feel the same way with my own horse." He glanced at the cart horse, and she chuckled. "No, not old Rumtum. Poor old fellow, he has worked so hard today and wants his dinner."

"That's something that can be soon remedied. If you will stand aside, Miss Linden, I'll push the cart out of the rut."

She looked relieved. "I did not want to presume, but—could you, possibly? It is a great imposition, and the cart is very heavy, but if we work together, we can manage."

It was on the tip of Harcourt's tongue to say that pushing a cart was not a woman's work, but his words died away as he looked down at the determined little lady beside him.

"It is," she pointed out, "my cart."

Nella liked Major Harcourt's smile. It was open and frank and warmed his gray eyes. He did not patronize her or look at her with the sly, speculative way that many gentlemen affected. "Well, Miss Linden, I will take this end of the cart. You lead your horse."

"But that means you will have to do all the hard work," she objected.

"I think you will be more effective leading your horse than pushing."

Her laugh was delightful, Harcourt noted, and quite unlike the simpers and twitters of fashionable debs. "You mean that I am puny, do you not? Very well, I will follow your orders, sir."

Pluck to the backbone, Harcourt approved as the little lady caught Rumtum's reins and coaxed him forward.

Nella had expected that it would take some time to free the cart, but she had underestimated Major Harcourt's strength. One heave, and the wheel was dislodged; the cart was free.

"Thank you," she cried. "I do not know what we would have done without your help. You are very strong, sir."

He was also very dirty. With dismay, Nella noted that his dark gray frock coat and tan breeches were covered with dust and she realized for the first time that Major Charles Harcourt was not dressed for riding. It was as if he had thrown saddle and bridle on his bay and come out on a whim.

She understood this feeling well. Many times along the years, she had had a sudden, compelling urge to leave her duties behind her and gallop free through the meadows. She had meant to take Excalibur out this morning, but there had been so much to do, and it was also market day. Stubbs was much too old, and the March rains had set Torfy's back to aching, and Mrs. Brunce could not drive a cart.

"I am sorry about your clothes," she said contritely. "Is there something I can do to make amends?" He shook his head, smiling, and she added, "Surely there is some way I can thank you."

As Harcourt took the small, white hand she held out, he noted that there were hard calluses under her second and third fingers. "Are you sure you'll be all right going home?" he asked.

Nella was warmed by the genuine concern in his voice. "Indeed I will. Linden House is not far from here, and it is such a fine day that I will enjoy the drive."

He helped her onto the seat of the cart and handed her her whip and glove. Then he bowed, stepped back, and whistled for his horse. Nella's eyes glowed with pleasure as the handsome bay came trotting up to lay his head on his master's shoulder.

"He is perfect," she breathed. "My father once had a mare of that exact coloring."

Another man might not have noticed the slight shift in her voice, but Harcourt caught it at once. It didn't take much to guess that the bay mare was no longer in her possession.

A lady who'd come upon hard times, who was forced to do her own marketing and housework as well—he'd known many such. What made Nella Linden different was that she made no bones about it.

"I must be getting back or Angel will begin to worry," she was saying.

"Is Angel your older sister?"

Nella shook her head. "She is my stepmama."

A stepmother. Harcourt had an unpleasant vision of a harpy like Lady Portwick and was silent as he watched Nella gather up the reins and her whip.

The small, capable hands were now gloved, the calluses hidden. She was undoubtedly going back to drudgery, but her farewell wave was jaunty, and her back, as she drove the old cart away, was as straight as a lance.

Harcourt almost sighed as he watched her go. A pity, he thought. It was too bad that a splendid girl like that had to be poor.

Poverty, Nella thought, had one advantage. Though Angelica might deplore the fact that she and her stepdaughters were forced to wear thrice-turned gowns, Nella herself felt freer than she had in the days when she was compelled to change her clothes every time she came in or went out.

The irony of the thought made Nella smile wryly. Then, her smile faded as she passed the stable. Once this long, slope-roofed building had housed at least ten blood horses, which had been attended to by three jockeys, no less than four grooms, and five undergrooms. Now, only Rumtum and Excalibur were left, and the stables had a mournful, dispirited look.

Turning her back on the stables, Nella walked up to the riding track. No battle on the Peninsula was as ruthless as the war Torfy carried on against the weeds on that track, but he was only one man, and the once-smooth track was beginning to be infested with crabgrass. Even so, nothing could lessen the splendor of the sleek, black horse that was grazing in the paddock beside the track.

Excalibur neighed a greeting, and the bent-over

form of Torfy came limping out of the stables. "You should be abed," Nella called out to him. "You know that your back will only become worse if you try to work."

"Nay, Miss Nella, the day tha' can find me abed is the day I die," Torfy whispered.

Nella was used to Torfy's die-away method of speech. Tall and rangy, red-faced, raw-boned and fierce-eyed, the Yorkshireman was as shy as a wild fox. He had been part of Linden House almost as long as old Stubbs himself and had risen from a lowly horse boy to become chief trainer of Sir Tom's horses. Stony-faced, he had watched as these animals were sold to make good Sir Tom's debts at Newmarket, but Nella knew that each sale had torn away a piece of Torfy's heart.

And that heart was loyalty itself. As they walked together to the paddock, Nella recalled that Torfy could have had almost any position he wanted after Sir Tom died. She knew for sure of four excellent offers the trainer had had, but he had refused them all, choosing to stay at Linden House for starvation wages and incredible amounts of work. Partly this was because of his feelings for the family, and partly, everyone suspected, it was because Torfy's soul burned with unspoken love for the tart-tongued Welsh housekeeper, Mrs. Brunce.

They had reached the paddock, and Excalibur came to Nella swiftly, dipping his soft muzzle into her shoulder. She stroked the horse's proud, arched neck, thinking that he was as sleek as warm ebony. An almost painful love filled Nella's heart.

"Excalibur is the fastest horse we've ever raised, isn't he?" she murmured.

"Nigh on, Miss Nella. He's faster nor his sire, Merlin, and he has more brains than his grandsire, Lancelot. A gradely horse is our Excalibur. We're never going to have to sell him?" Torfy whispered anxiously.

"Not if I can help it."

"I know things are bad, Miss Nella," Torfy sighed. "Nay, since the master's death, it's been one thing after another."

She turned to look into fierce, worried eyes and tried to smile. "We can face only one day at a time."

"That's true, Miss Nella. But now—"

She interrupted. "Now I think I will exercise Excalibur."

She insisted on saddling the stallion herself. Then, mounting, she tapped her heels on Excalibur's flanks. Not needing further urging, the ebony horse sprang forward. Around the riding track they went, so swiftly that Nella felt as though they were flying.

This was how Major Harcourt must feel when he rode his Lancer. Nella's concentration, till now wholly on Excalibur, suddenly faltered.

She scolded herself for her foolishness. This was no time to think of smiling gray eyes is a sun-darkened face. There was Lady Portwick's ball to face and Excalibur to protect. Yet, in spite of all her common sense, Nella could not help wishing that today, when she had met Major Harcourt, she had been riding Excalibur and not driving the old market cart.

# Chapter Three

Nella and Rosemary watched in admiration as Mrs. Brunce arranged a circlet of pearls and forget-me-nots in their stepmother's hair. The pearls were paste, and the silk flowers had graced an old bonnet, but the effect was still stunning.

"There, my lady," Mrs. Brunce exclaimed. "Let the girls look at you, now then."

Self-conscious, but anxious to please, Angelica rose to her feet. She did indeed look breathtakingly lovely in her ball gown of pale blue gossamer satin embroidered with tiny silver flowers. The amethyst brocade sash around her waist exactly matched the color of her eyes as did her satin slippers. The almost, but not quite, scandalous dip of her decolletage revealed the creamy pallor of her skin.

"Stand just like that, Angel, or I will lose the light on your face." Rosemary had whipped out her sketchbook and was busily sketching. "Chiaroscuro is very important, you know."

Obediently, Angelica stood quite still. Mrs. Brunce folded long arms across a bony bosom and clicked her tongue. "*Ach y fy,* Miss Rosa. Put away that old sketchbook, now then. Brunce do have to get you ready for the ball."

"Bruncie, if you do not stop squeezing your mouth up like a goldfish, I will put you in the sketch, too," Rosemary warned. "And I will show the sketch to Torfy."

A faint blush stained the Welshwoman's gaunt cheeks. "Mind your tongue, Miss Rosa," she scolded. "As if I'd look twice at that timid fool of a man."

While she grumbled, Nella walked slowly around her stepmother. "You have done wonders, Bruncie," she declared, and indeed no one would suspect that the brocade for the sash and the material for the satin shoes had been cannibalized from Nella's only surviving evening dress and cloak.

Angelica was beautiful, desirable, and for all the world knew, she was exquisitely gowned. Nella exulted, "Angel, you will be the loveliest lady at the ball."

Angelica's cheeks became almost painfully pink, and she twisted her hands together nervously. "I cannot help but feel that I am unsuitably dressed. Sir Tom has only been dead a year—"

"Sir Tom," Nella interrupted, "would say that you were a great gun."

Mrs. Brunce sniffed disapprovingly. "It is not seemly to use your poor father's cant expressions, Miss Nella. Miss Rosa, will you stop that pen scratching and let me attend to your toilet?"

She advanced on Rosemary, then stopped to look at what the girl had drawn. Her long face softened; her grim mouth relaxed. "You've caught her ladyship to the life, Miss Rosa, my little one. But you haven't the time to paint now, see? The hired carriage will be coming for you, now just."

With an impatient sigh, Rosemary put down her sketchbook and got to her feet. "It doesn't matter. I have nothing to wear, and you can't make *me* look beautiful anyway."

As Mrs. Brunce prodded Rosemary out of the room, Angelica murmured in a stricken voice, "Neither of you have pretty clothes because you cut up your dresses to make mine."

Gently, so as not to disturb Angelica's dress, Nella hugged her stepmother. "Collect, dear goose, why we are going to this odious ball. You are the one who *must* look beautiful. Rosa and I have very suitable clothing."

She held her arms wide to show off the brown cambric gown she wore. It was as neat as wax, and its round neck was brave with lace. Mrs. Brunce had stitched up the sleeves cleverly so that worn places would not show and had added more lace across the bodice and around the hem. The problem was that the dress was more suitable for an afternoon's walking-out than for Lady Portwick's ball.

There was the sound of wrangling in the other room, and Mrs. Brunce exclaimed, "Oh, dammo, will you not sit still? You act as though you had a hundred old fleas with you."

Angelica looked shocked. She was a little afraid of Mrs. Brunce and her tart tongue, but Nella paid little attention. Both she and Rosemary were used to being bullied as well as loved and protected by the gaunt Welshwoman who had come to Linden House as a young widow and had been their nurse, their housekeeper, and was now their cook as well as their woman of all work. Together with old Stubbs, she was the only one who had stayed on when the other servants left.

"You must not mind Bruncie," she told Angelica. "She has the kindest heart and only flies up into the boughs because she is worried about us."

"With good reason," Angelica murmured. "Nella, are you sure that this is wise?"

Nella's reply was lost as Mrs. Brunce stormed in with Rosemary in tow. "Miss Nella, see if you can persuade this old mule of a girl to behave."

Rosemary's mouth was pushed out into a mutinous pout. "I won't go to the ball like this. I look like a leg of mutton."

The description was somewhat apt. Mrs. Brunce had laced Rosemary into a maroon dress of jaconet muslin with buttons down the front. It was a good enough dress but much too tight.

"If I take a breath or eat anything, the buttons will pop off," Rosemary complained.

"Then don't breathe and don't eat," Mrs. Brunce replied promptly. "Ladies do not go to balls to stuff themselves."

Rosemary looked horrified. "Of course I am going to eat," she cried. "Why else would I go to that horrid woman's house?"

Mrs. Brunce lost her temper and began to shout in Welsh. Rosemary insisted that she was going to stay home. Just then Stubbs creaked upstairs to announce, "The hired carriage has arrived, m'lady."

His face was carefully bland, but his voice fairly oozed unhappiness that the family should have fallen on such evil days that it could not afford decent conveyence of its own. Nella acted swiftly before more gloom descended on the evening.

"Excellent," she said briskly. "He is on time. Rosa, are you aware that Lord Portwick's late father was a much regarded collector of art? I am persuaded that there will be a great deal to interest you at Portwick Hall. Angel, here is your pelisse."

With a deep sigh Angelica accepted a pelisse trimmed with downy feathers. Mrs. Brunce had haunted the local poulter's for days in order to assemble the garment, but Angelica did not seem to appreciate this. In fact, she looked so miserable that even Nella's stout heart sank.

Silently, the Linden ladies followed a grim Mrs. Brunce and a doleful Stubbs down to the courtyard. It was drizzling, and neither the hired carriage or its driver looked impressive.

Wrapping her own old cloak around her, Nella summoned every ounce of cheer she had. "Well," she said, "we are off to the ball at last."

Rosemary sniffed. Angelica climbed into the carriage as though it were a tumbril sent to convey her to her doom. Nella thought, I hope I am not making a mistake.

She had had her doubts about her scheme these past days, but she had kept them to herself. She had told herself that no other course was open to them. There were few options for well-born females who had fallen upon hard times. Lacking a moneyed gentleman to marry, a lady might languish in genteel poverty, depend on the charity of unwilling relatives, or try and eke out starvation wages as a governess or lady's companion.

And even these meager options were not open to Nella's family. The Lindens had no living relatives, and Angelica's only hope was a sour older sister who had married the son of a country squire and lived in Derbyshire. Nella was already doing her best to earn her bread by giving riding lessons and boarding horses. And poverty was not genteel.

She thought of this as the hired carriage rumbled over the few miles that separated Linden House from the Portwicks' residence, but her resolution faltered when they arrived at the gates of Portwick Hall. These huge iron gates, flung open on this festive night, seemed to sneer at anyone so wanting in ton as to come to a ball in a hired hack.

Everything about Portwick Hall seemed to breathe opulence tonight. Jealous of her reputation as an excellent hostess, Lady Portwick had caused a thick, crimson carpet to flow through the open front door, down marble steps, and across the gravel of the courtyard. A canopy made of cloth of gold had been stretched over the carpet so that guests need not be exposed to the fine drizzle. Footmen in gorgeous livery and snow-white wigs hurried to set down carriage steps so that guests could descend. A faint sound of music filled the misty air.

"We are here," Nella said unnecessarily. "Look,

there is a footman to set down our step. Heart up, Angel."

She broke off as the underfootman who had been hurrying their way came to a stop. Another carriage had just pulled up, and this one sported a ducal crest. Instantly the footman raced off to attend to the more important guest.

"We do not belong here," Angel said in a small, tight voice. "Nella, *please* let us go home."

"Fustian. We were invited." Nella clasped her small, gloved hand on the reticule that held the precious invitation as she added, "We are as good as anyone else. *You* are much more beautiful than any female present. Keep your head high, and damn the enemy."

Quoting Sir Tom's favorite saying did its work. Rosemary giggled and Angelica almost smiled. Nella leaned out of the carriage door, spied a footman some distance away, and called peremptorily, "You, there! Come here at once and assist us."

Nella's tone was haughty, her bearing imperious. Galvanized by these indications of Quality, the footman obeyed, and soon the Linden ladies were walking up the crimson carpet and through doors manned by no less than four bewigged menials. They then paused in the marble ground-level hallway and looked up at the red carpet that swept up to the first floor. Here an orchestra was playing for the enjoyment of the arriving guests.

Followed by her sister and stepmother, Nella walked up the stairs, passed the orchestra, and came to a halt before a dignified personage who could be none other than the Portwicks' butler.

Swift, knowing eyes flickered over the way Nella was dressed. He dismissed her as unimportant, dismissed Rosemary, and then came to Angelica. She was so beautiful that no man alive could dismiss *her*, and Angelica, though inwardly quaking, rose to the occasion.

"You may announce us," she said in her most dignified tone. "I am Lady Linden. These are my daughters, the Misses Linden."

The butler hastened to Angelica's bidding. The doors of the great drawing room were thrown open, and the Lindens swept in.

Nella's first impression was one of heat. After the economical chill that pervaded Linden House and the March coldness outside, the Portwick's drawing room felt like a hothouse. As though to complete this analogy, flowerlike ladies were posed gracefully everywhere. They stood by the marble fireplace, sat by the golden draperies that concealed the French windows, or beside their mamas and chaperons on ornate loveseats and sofas.

Through narrowed eyes, Nella assessed the competition. Though no woman present was as lovely as Angelica, she had to admit that all of Lady Portwick's female guests were exquisitely garbed. They wore dresses of the most daring decolletage, dresses of gauze over silk slips, cambric gowns with stiffened bodices to push up almost-bared breasts, or creations of China crêpe with the high hemlines of the current mode that showed neat ankles and even part of the calf.

And these dresses were made of jewel colors. Ruby, amethyst, pearl, emerald, amber, citrine, and ivory blazed in various shades and were reflected by the mirrors that lined the drawing room walls. Amid the sea of colors and the acreage of white, dimpled, scented skin, Nella felt like a dowd. She glanced at Rosemary, who was looking around her with round eyes, and then at Angelica. In this glittering company, would Angel even be noticed?

Several gentlemen had turned around to see who the latecomers were. Nella had an impression of more color—coats of blue and canary yellow, pink, and the scarlet of regimentals, before their host, his rotund form squeezed and corsetted into a frog-green swallow-tail coat, detached himself from the others and wavered over to them.

Though it was early in the evening, Lord Portwick's speech was already slightly slurred. "Welcome to Portwick Hall, my dear ladies," he exclaimed, then took Angelica's hand in his and pressed it meaningfully. "Lady Linden, your most obedient."

Angelica curtseyed and attempted unsuccessfully to withdraw her hand. Lord Portwick rambled on, "Sir Thomas was a dashed good friend of mine. Anything I can do for hish—his lovely widow, dear lady. Mean to say, dash it, you have only to ask."

He sighed boozily, and a gust of brandy-flavored air wafted over them all. Angelica looked pleadingly at Nella who said briskly, "How good you are, Lord Portwick. Perhaps you would be kind enough to introduce us to some of your guests? We have been in mourning for so long that we have lost touch with the outside world."

"Yes—quite—other guests." Reluctantly, Lord Portwick freed Angelica's hand and walked them forward. Next moment, they were making their curtseys to their hostess and to a fair, blue-eyed gentleman who attended her.

Lady Portwick was dressed in a costly gown of citrine-colored satin worn low on the shoulder to show a vastness of plump neck and bosom. Jewels were scattered across her bodice, and more adorned her turban. Her appearance almost eclipsed her companion, who was garbed in unexceptional black superfine, and Nella was astounded when he was introduced as the Earl of Deering.

Was *this* the infamous London rake? But rakes and reprobates should look cynical or wicked, while this man was young and handsome and had a friendly smile. He looked, Nella thought, no older than herself. Perhaps reports about his womanizing had been exaggerated.

Then, Nella saw the appraising look he was giving her stepmother. There was no mistaking the keen interest that flared in that blue gaze as he bowed over Angelica's hand.

Rake, she thought. Fox in the vineyard. Oh, Angel, take care!

Angelica's cheeks had pinkened delicately. "My lord," she murmured.

"Your servant, Lady Linden."

Nella's concern deepened. The earl had somehow transformed that commonplace, everyday speech into something personal, even intimate.

Fortunately, Lady Portwick had no intention of wasting her guest of honor on country nobodies. She threaded an arm through her brother's and said repressively, "It is good to see you, Lady Linden." She then pointedly turned away to add, "Is that the Viscount of Liens that I see at the door? Deering, I must make you known to their daughter, Miss Leigh."

"Odious woman," Nella muttered, as their hostess dragged the earl away. Even so, she was grateful that Lady Portwick had removed the earl. An innocent like Angel, Nella thought, would be easy prey for a seasoned man about town like Deering.

Her thoughts were interrupted as a few of their Hampshire neighbors came up to greet them. Among these was Lady Lake, whose unmarried son, the Honorable Percival Lake, begged an introduction. Though he was polite to Nella and Rosemary, he made it quite clear that it was Angelica he wanted to meet.

The Honorable Percival was only the first of Angelica's admirers. Other gentlemen clustered around her and soon, ensconced in a chair by the fire, she blushed and smiled and thoroughly enchanted her growing circle of cavaliers.

From the shadow of a large potted palm tree, Nella watched her stepmother's admirers multiply to include such diverse persons as Lord Moore, a landowner of much consequence, several band-box dandies, and Mr. Jared Hampton, a stolid, wealthy widower.

"Success," Nella breathed. "Thank heavens for Lady Portwick."

"Now that," a familiar voice beside her remarked, "is doing it too brown, ma'am."

Nella looked around quickly and found herself staring up into Major Charles Harcourt's smiling gray eyes. She had not expected to see him again, and certainly not at Lady Portwick's ball. Her heart gave a quiver that must have been the result of her surprise.

The major was dressed in his regimentals, which suited his hard, sun-bronzed features. His eyes kept their smile as he added, "I can't imagine anyone giving thanks for that abominable woman."

Her first emotion had been surprise—and pleasure—at seeing him again. Her second thought was that the major had again caught her at a disadvantage. For a split second Nella regretted the sacrifice of her one brocade and satin dress.

Then she shook off such idiotish thoughts. "Everyone," she pointed out, "has some good in them." Major Harcourt's dark eyebrow rose quizzically. "Collect that she *did* invite us to her ball."

"I'm sure that her motives were vile. Still, I'm delighted that you are here."

Another man might have made that speech flirtatious, or insinuating, or bold. Major Harcourt sounded as though he meant every word he said.

"If you dislike Lady Portwick so much, why are you here?" she wondered aloud.

Ruefully he explained, "The devil of it is that I'm a guest in her house. I came down to Hampshire with Deering."

Nella followed the major's gaze and was unpleasantly surprised to see that Deering had joined the group around Angelica.

"The earl and I served together on the Peninsula," the major was saying. "We became friends."

"You must be a *very* good friend to come down *here* with him." When he laughed, Nella added penitently, "I beg your pardon. Sir Tom used to tell me that my tongue would land me in the briars."

"Nonsense. You are merely being honest." Harcourt looked down at the diminutive Miss Nella Linden and realized that he *was* glad she was there. He had been bored by Lady Portwick's male guests, who had taken pains to tell him exactly how the war with Napoleon *should* have been fought. The ladies in their costly gowns with their simpering ways and bold eyes had not interested him. In fact, Harcourt had been about to escape when Nella and her companions had arrived.

"Who is Sir Tom?" he asked.

"He is—was—my father." Harcourt saw a shadow touch Nella's eyes as she continued, "He died last January. Angel—Lady Linden, I mean—is his widow."

Harcourt was astonished. The beauty with her golden curls and blue eyes looked almost younger than Nella herself. Sir Tom had apparently robbed the cradle.

As though she had read his mind, Nella said, "Angel is a darling." Realizing that she sounded somewhat defensive she added, "She is so beautiful, and so sweet and so *shy* that my younger sister Rosa and I loved her at once. Sir Tom saved her, you know, from marriage with an old rake."

"Aha."

"An old rake who *drooled*," Nella said sternly. "It was not cream-pot love for Sir Tom. He felt sorry for Angel."

Harcourt glanced cynically at the crowd around the fair young widow and was not surprised to see that Deering had managed to push himself close to her chair. Nella, following the direction of the major's eyes, felt agitated. She wondered if she should go up to Angelica and foil the rake's plans.

Harcourt wondered why Nella looked so uneasy and decided that she was unhappy because her stepmother was receiving so much attention.

"I am surprised that a lady as beautiful as Lady Linden has not remarried," he said smoothly.

Before Nella could answer, the orchestra that Lady Portwick had hired entered the drawing room. Under the guidance of the conductor, they arranged themselves in a corner and commenced to play.

Like flowers unfolding, the glittering personages in the drawing room began to drift toward the center of the floor. Lord Portwick led his lady forward, and smiling ladies gave their hands to bowing partners. There was a slight stir in the group about Angelica as she allowed Deering to lead her to the floor.

Harcourt noted the unhappy look deepen in Nella's green eyes. Why not? he thought.

Bowing slightly he asked, "Might I have the honor of this dance, Miss Linden?"

To his astonishment, she shook her head. "I thank you, but no. I have never been much good at dancing. In fact, Sir Tom used to say that I was of no use except with a whip in my fist or on the back of a horse."

When she spoke of horses, her face was suddenly transformed. Harcourt was unprepared for the enthusiasm that brightened Nella's green eyes to emerald and gave her face an almost luminous beauty. He felt slightly dazzled, as though he had looked too deep into the heart of a flame.

With difficulty he concentrated on what she was saying. "Sir Tom taught me to ride himself, he and Torfy, our groom and trainer. I never had a pony—it was up on the back of a full-grown mare, and after that a hunter. My Thunder could take every fence."

Nella stopped, surprised at herself. She had not thought of Thunder for a long time. There was no use in remembering—or in boring the major.

But the major did not looked bored. "I can see why you would prefer to ride than dance," he said.

"Do you? But you see—" Nella broke off in midsentence as the minuet ended and a waltz began. Instead of giving way to the grave Lord Moore, who was advancing purposefully on Angelica, Deering was once again sweeping her toward the floor. Nella frowned as the earl took Angelica's white hand in his and put an arm around her waist.

"I have heard that the waltz is an immodest dance," she murmured.

Harcourt suddenly understood Nella's concern. The girl was actually playing chaperon for her stepmother. "I assure you it is quite respectable," he said. "Would you like me to show you?"

As she looked up into the major's smiling gray eyes, Nella forgot all about Angel being swirled about in the arms of a rake. The thought of having the major's strong arm around her waist was both exciting and inviting. For an instant, she was actually tempted to put her hand in his, but good sense came to her rescue.

She did not know how to waltz. She would make a cake of herself in front of Lady Portwick and all her guests. Besides, she had not come to the ball to dance with the major. She and Rosa were there merely as companions for Angelica. . . .

With a spurt of guilt, Nella realized that she had not seen Rosemary for some time. In fact, she had forgotten all about her younger sister.

"No, I thank you," she told the major. "I beg that you will excuse me. I must see how my younger sister is getting on."

As Harcourt bowed and walked on, Nella looked about the drawing room. She could not see her sister anywhere, and her guilt increased. Rosemary in her too-tight dress must be suffering agonies of hunger. Also, unused to social affairs such as this, she must be most uncomfortable.

Perhaps she was hiding? Nella edged close toward the golden drapes nearest her and glanced behind them as discreetly as she could. There was no one there, and a dowager seated nearby put up her lorgnette in disapproval. Hurriedly, Nella moved away to continue her search. Could Rosemary be behind the potted palm by the door? No. Outside the drawing room, then, in the hall?

There was no one in the hall or on the stairs. Attempting not to be too obvious, Nella strolled down the carpeted hallway and opened the first door she found. It was empty. In the second room she found a snoring old gentleman, and in the third she surprised a couple who were kissing each other enthusiastically. Hurriedly, Nella closed the door on them and stood wondering what she should do next.

Could the madcap have decided to go home? After all, Rosa had hated the idea of coming to the ball. Nella picked up her skirts, ran down the stairs to the ground floor, and ignoring the surprised footmen, went outdoors.

It was cold outside and the earlier rain had become a heavy fog that enveloped the waiting coaches and made them appear dim and ghostly. Nella had to feel her way from one coach to the other until she found the one that they had hired for the evening.

It was still there. Since it was too far to walk back to Linden House, Rosemary must be somewhere about. Wishing that she could see through the fog, Nella began to walk back to the house but mistook her way. Gravel turned underfoot, then became rain-smooth grass.

"I am in a garden," Nella mused aloud.

"Miss Linden?" a surprised voice inquired.

Gravel scrunched underfoot as Major Harcourt walked toward her. "I escaped to fortify myself with a cigar, I confess," he said, "but it's miserably damp."

There was a question in his deep voice, and Nella felt impelled to explain, "I am searching for my younger sister. She seems to have disappeared."

Harcourt tossed his cigar into some bushes. "It's no night for a lady to be out walking," he remarked. "You could have sent a servant to search for your sister."

He sounded so kind and concerned that Nella decided to trust him with the truth. "Rosa is not used to gatherings such as this. She did not want to come to the ball, and she might be hiding from all these people. Or, perhaps, she is in raptures over some work of art somewhere. I wanted to be the one who found her, not the servants."

"I know the house rather well. Let me help you find her," Harcourt said and was touched by Nella's relief.

He escorted her back to the house, sternly quelled the surprised look the footmen gave them, then said, "Your sister is fond of art, you say? In that case, let's try the gallery first."

Laughter and music followed them up a winding stairs to a well-lit second floor. "Morning room, Green Saloon," Harcourt mused, "and here's the gallery."

He flung open a door disclosing a cavernous room, dimly lit by candles. The room was practically crammed with statues and portraits of every description, but the room was deserted.

Nella did not even try to hide her disappointment.

"I was sure she would be here. Where else could the tiresome child have gone?"

She turned to leave the room and then stood, transfixed, staring at an enormous canvas that hung on one wall. It depicted a knight wearing the red cross of the crusader.

"Who is that?" Nella gasped.

Her tone held a note of awe. Harcourt replied, "That, dear lady, is the legendary Saint Hugh, the crusader from whom Lady Portwick claims to have descended."

"Oh, not him," Nella interrupted. "I meant the horse."

There was no doubt that the artist had loved horses. He had painted a coal-black stallion with a long, beautifully arched neck, a small, neat head, and large, intelligent eyes. One perfectly formed foreleg was lifted as though the painted animal might at any moment come cantering out into the gallery.

"He is the image of Excalibur," Nella breathed.

Harcourt looked at her and saw, for the second time that night, the luminous quality in her shining green eyes. He also noted that her mouth was soft and sweet and invited kissing.

The need to kiss Nella Linden came out of nowhere and struck him with the force of a blow to the solar plexus. Harcourt actually found himself breathless as he looked down at that vivid, bright face.

It took a supreme act of will to pull himself together. "Excalibur," he repeated. "Your horse, I think?"

"Yes. I have told you about him, but I do not think that I told you that he descends from the finest bloodline—from Dark Merlin out of Guinevere. When her time came, Sir Tom attended her himself. Torfy and I helped. Oh, you should have seen him when he was foaled. All eyes and legs and still as handsome as a young prince."

As she spoke, Nella turned toward the major. More words of praise for Excalibur were on her lips, but when she saw the look in Harcourt's eyes, she fell silent.

Nella felt as though her heart had suddenly stopped in mid-beat. She caught her breath and drew into her lungs the pleasant scent of the major's cigar and of leather and cool mist. She felt as though she herself were enveloped in that mist. Even the ground beneath her feet no longer felt solid. Involuntarily, she took a step toward Harcourt just as he took a step toward her.

Suddenly, the door of the gallery crashed open. "*There* you are, Nella," Rosemary cried.

# Chapter Four

PINK-CHEEKED AND PLEASED with herself, Rosemary fairly bounced into the gallery. "I have been wondering where you were," she cried. "Nella, Lionel has been showing me the most *delicious* art that his late grandfather collected. I am persuaded Portwick Hall is more interesting than the Louvre."

In the dim light of the gallery, Nella had not noted that Rosemary was accompanied by a gentleman. Now she recognized Lady Portwick's only son. She recalled that many years ago, when Lady Elizabeth had still been alive, Lady Portwick had occasionally visited Linden House. In those days Lionel and Rosemary, then both barely out of leading strings, had played together.

Even as a baby, Lionel had been under his mother's thumb, and he had hero-worshipped the chubby, free-spirited Rosemary. He was now almost a man, and the padded shoulders of his new evening coat of blue superfine gave him the illusion of maturity, but the look of puplike devotion in his eyes was familiar.

"Now, really, Rosa," he protested, "that's not true."

"Yes, it is," Rosemary retorted, "only, I am sure

that the Louvre would take *much* better care of its treasures."

Relief and exasperation struggled within Nella. "We have been searching everywhere for you, Rosa."

The uncorrigible girl did not even hear. "Would you believe it, Nella? Lady Portwick does not seem to care about her beautiful works of art. There is a Van Dyke that is covered with fly specks and a Hogarth in a mildewed frame! And there was a still life of apples and grapes which—but that reminds me, I am fearfully hungry."

Aware that Harcourt was listening with keen interest, Nella interrupted. "Rosa, this is Major Harcourt, who kindly helped me look for you. Major, this is my younger sister, Rosemary."

For so large a man, Nella thought, the major executed a very graceful bow. Then he smiled at Lionel. "Well, lad. I see you've found a fellow artist."

Lionel blushed. "Rosa—I mean, Miss Rosemary—is much more gifted than I ever could be, sir. I'm a mere smatterer next to her." He paused, reddened even further, and stammered, "Good evening, Miss Linden. I haven't seen you since Sir Tom—I mean, since your father—that is to say, I'm most awfully sorry. . . ."

His words trailed away, and Nella said gently, "I know what you mean to say, and thank you. I am grateful that you kept Rosa company."

Before Lionel could answer, Rosemary bubbled, "It is not true that you are a smatterer, Lionel. Nella, he has shown me his sketchings, and they are excellent! It is too bad that he must keep his light under a bushel. Lord Portwick is usually on the toodle and does not care what Lionel does, but his mama considers painting an unsuitable occupation for a gentleman. And that is purest fudge, since all the old masters were men. There is Michelangelo and Raphael, and that Dutchman who always painted his mistresses unclothed."

Hurriedly Nella interposed, "This is no time for a lesson in art, Rosa."

But Rosemary had discovered the portrait of Sir Hugh. She walked over to it and looked at it critically. "I collect that this is the legendary ancestor that Lady Portwick is so proud of. He looks a proper sapskull, but the horse is magnificent. And, oh, the gilt frame is starting to peel. I should think your mama would do something about it, Lionel."

"I've told her, but she won't listen," Lionel sighed. "Mama is not concerned with art."

As he went to stand beside Rosemary, Harcourt commented, "I'm glad that the lad has found a friend."

He had spoken idly, but Nella looked somber. "Lady Portwick would never allow a friendship between her son and the Lindens."

Meaning that Lady Portwick was rich and the Lindens were poor. There was a dry twist to Harcourt's fine lips, but he remained silent.

Nella turned to look at him earnestly. "You must not think that I am complaining. We cannot change the cards that we are given, and we must play them as best we can. Angel says—"

She stopped short, and a stricken look filled her

eyes. "I had forgotten about Angel! We must return to the drawing room at once."

Hastily she shepherded her sister out of the gallery, and the men followed. As they descended the stairs to the strains of music and merriment, they found two young ladies promenading in the hallway under the watchful eye of their chaperon. They bowed cooly to the Linden ladies, smiled at Lionel, and fluttered their eyelashes and costly fans in Harcourt's direction.

"Silly cats," Rosemary observed scornfully. "Acting like diamonds of the first water when they are only squabs."

"You know them?" Harcourt wondered.

Nella sent Rosemary a quelling look. "The blond lady is Lady Leigh and the dark one the Honorable Miss Vervain. Their estates lie not far away from here."

Harcourt recalled that Lady Portwick had mentioned them to Deering, hinting that both were of impeccable lineage and considerably plump of purse. A man could do worse, he thought idly as he followed Nella and Rosemary into the drawing room.

No one even looked up at their entrance. Angelica was dancing the cotillion with Lord Moore, Lady Portwick was deep in conversation with a group of matrons, and Deering was partnering a dark-haired young lady in a low-cut gown of emerald crêpe embroidered with pearls.

"Oh, that is all right, then," Nella murmured in relief. "Lord Moore is a very correct gentleman."

"Forgive my curiosity," Harcourt said, "but why

do you feel that you must chaperon your stepmother?"

"You mean that it should be the other way around? I suppose that I am by nature a managing female. Sir Tom used to say so."

"Sir Tom was a fortunate man."

He had spoken abruptly, and she turned to look up at him. His face was bland, but there was an unfamiliar, hard look in his eyes. Suddenly unsure of herself she said slowly, "He lost my mother early, you know. They loved each other very much, and I think that it was her loss that caused him to bet so heavily at Newmarket."

"Naturally," Harcourt murmured.

Nella's delicate brows puckered into a thoughtful frown. "When our mother died, Rosa was barely out of leading strings. I was ten. Of course I tried to help Sir Tom as best I could."

What she meant was that the running of the household had fallen on her young shoulders. Harcourt though several harsh things about the late Sir Tom before remarking, "And now you are helping his widow. A natural progression of things."

Nella did not like the major's tone. "Angel needs to be protected. She had such a sad life with her family, for they never loved her. We," Nella continued, "were always loved."

"But can one live on love alone?"

The cynical question made her speak without thinking. "Of course not! That is why Angel must make a good match this time, and—"

Horrified at what she had blurted out, Nella broke

off just as Lord Portwick rolled forward to announce, "Shtop the music. Time for shup—supper. Gentlemen, pleash to take your ladies to the dining room."

Lord Portwick's speech was most slurred, and his gait was unsteady as he perambulated to her ladyship and offered her his arm. "Come, m'sweet," he chortled. "Have to show the dashed flag. Gotter lead the way to food and drink. Specially drink, that's the ticket."

Lady Portwick could not fall out with her lord in public, but she glared at him and took his arm in a manner that did not bode well for the future. Then, her eyes narrowed as she saw that her brother was walking across the room to offer his arm to Lady Angelica Linden.

How could Deering forget himself so thoroughly as to take an impoverished widow in to dinner? Lady Portwick was outraged, especially because she had specifically instructed her sheep-brained brother to afford Lady Leigh the courtesy of dinner. Then, to her added horror, she saw that Lionel was standing beside that hurly-burly chit, Rosemary Linden.

Her son was actually going to offer his arm to Rosemary Linden. It was more than flesh and blood could stand. "Lionel!" Lady Portwick hissed.

Her penetrating whisper caused her son and heir to jerk upright. "M-mama?" he stammered.

In a voice that dripped vinegar, the lady directed, "Please to take Lady Leigh in to supper, my son."

Lionel glanced helplessly at Rosemary, who shrugged. "Best do as your mama says, Lionel," she acceded cheerfully. "She looks as mad as fire."

Nella winced. A lady standing nearby giggled. Lady Portwick fairly swelled and sent Rosemary a glare that would have reduced a mountain to sand. Astonished at such hostility, Rosemary gasped. As she exhaled, one of the buttons on her too-tight bodice detached itself.

She clapped her hand to her bosom, and two other buttons snapped off. Like projectiles, they flew though the air. One landed harmlessly on the carpet, but its mate scored a direct hit on the advancing Lady Portwick's generous bosom. The lady uttered a loud gasp as the offending button slid down her decolletage and fell onto the ground.

Angelica looked horrified. Deering grinned. There were sniggers from several of the gentlemen standing nearby. Scarlet with mortification, Rosemary moved forward to retrieve her buttons, but Nella was quicker. Kneeling, she reached to pick up the buttons.

"Insufferable! *Will* you get out of the way?" Lady Portwick snarled.

Nella looked up into the lady's suffused face and tried to form some kind of apology. No words came. Mutely, she straightened to allow Lady Portwick to sweep past.

As the other guests followed, Harcourt came to stand beside her. As though nothing had happened, he asked, "Shall we go in to dinner?"

For once embarassed, Rosemary covered her face with her hands. "I have just shamed poor Lionel and made a perfect guy of myself," she moaned. "Nella, please, can't we go home now?"

"If you do, you will only give that woman more ammunition," Harcourt pointed out. "It's wise to present your face to the enemy, ma'am, not your back."

Lifting her eyes, Nella met the major's quizzical gaze. Then, she stiffened her shoulders. "Rosa, we are going in to dinner. We are going in *now*, and damn the enemy."

Harcourt's eyes glinted with laughter, but he merely offered Nella his right arm. She took it defiantly. He then offered his left arm to Rosemary, who was already looking more cheerful.

"At any rate," she consoled herself, "now that those plaguey buttons are out of the way, I will be able to eat as much as I want."

"Your behavior, my lord, invites scandal," Lady Portwick proclaimed. "I cannot understand how you can eat as though nothing had happened."

The Earl of Deering, who had helped himself to kidneys, eggs, and ham, continued to eat his breakfast. His sister watched in fulminating silence for a few moments before charging, "You danced with that woman twice and you did not dance even *once* with Lady Leigh."

"Antidote, b'dad. Looks like a horse."

"How dare you say so?" Lady Portwick continued angrily. "And you also ignored Miss Vervain. And then to take that woman in to supper against my express wishes—"

"Stop calling her 'that woman,'" Deering interrupted testily. "She's got a name. Besides, you invited Lady Linden and her stepdaughters to your ball."

Lady Portwick cast up her pale blue eyes. "It was my Christian duty to do so, although with such a reprobate as Sir Thomas for a father, many feel that the Lindens are beneath the pale."

Lionel twitched like a rabbit. Harcourt looked up from his plate to remark, "How so?"

Lady Portwick recalled that last night the major had actually had the temerity to escort both Linden sisters in to dinner. The look that she gave him had been known to reduce grown men to trembling incoherence, but apparently it had no effect on the major. After a moment she said severely, "I collect that you do not know the family's history. Far be it for me to cast aspersions against my less fortunate neighbors, but Sir Thomas Linden was a gamester who lost his fortune at Newmarket. And there is worse."

"Do not tell me that Sir Thomas was also a confirmed drunkard," Harcourt exclaimed.

His deep voice was as smooth as silk, but Lady Portwick observed that the major was looking at her husband's vacant seat. She spoke through her teeth. "Sir Thomas Linden was a selfish, do-nothing spendthrift. That is why his widow and his daughters are forced to live in poverty."

" 'Blessed are the poor in spirit,' " Harcourt interrupted sententiously. "But you, as a Christian woman, would know that."

Lady Portwick changed her tactics. With a martyred sigh she said, "I try to be charitable, Major.

But what can one say of a young woman who so forgets herself as to act like a cit? Miss Citronella Linden fancies herself a horse trainer. She boards horses at Linden House and gives riding lessons. I am sure you did not know that."

"No," Harcourt said, "I did not know it. But I confess that I am not surprised."

"Nothing that that family does surprises *me*." Warming to the subject, Lady Portwick continued, "As to Rosemary Linden, she is so brass faced that she would tie her garter in public, as the saying goes."

"Mama, you are being too harsh," Lionel protested.

At this unusual show of spirit, Deering looked astounded, and Harcourt, who had risen from the table, turned around to stare. Lionel continued desperately, "Miss Rosemary is an artist. She has so many ideas, Mama, about—"

"A Bohemian," Lady Portwick interrupted. "She undoubtedly has the morals that go with that low type of person."

"Now that is intriguing," Harcourt exclaimed. "I did not expect to meet any Bohemians in Hampshire, did you, Deering? Ma'am, you've convinced me. I am going to ride to Linden House and pay my respects to Lady Linden and her stepdaughters."

Deering slapped his hand on the table. "B'dad, Court," he grinned, "I'll go with you. Got to visit Miss Cinderella—odd name, give you m'word—and her peerless stepmother."

Taking advantage of Lady Portwick's stunned silence, the men bowed and left the room. In the hall, Deering fairly crowed. "Piqued, repiqued, and capoted! That was well played, Court! Don't know how you keep Maria in check—nobody else can."

"Least of all that young cub of hers." Harcourt's eyes were suddenly grave as he added, "If he were my nephew, I'd do something to free him from those apron ties. They will strangle him, Ned."

" 'Struth, but there's nothing I can do. Face cavalry charges gladly, give you m'word, but I draw the line with Maria. Rather be flayed alive than cross *her*."

But as footmen ran to order the earl's curricle saddled, there were hurried footsteps behind them. "Uncle Edward, Major Harcourt," Lionel called breathlessly, "may I come with you to Linden House?"

Both men turned to stare at the flushed youth. "D'you mean to say," the earl exclaimed, "that m'sister has agreed to let you accompany us?"

"Mama thinks I am studying. What she don't know won't hurt her." The color heightened in the boy's cheeks as he pleaded, "Please let me come with you."

"Well, why not?" Harcourt threw an approving arm around the stripling's narrow shoulders. "You can drive with Deering, and I'll ride. Lancer hasn't had his morning run."

After last night's drizzle, the capricious March weather had gentled into a fitful sunshine, but as they skirted the lush meadowland that lay between Portwick Hall and Linden House, a mist lay fairly close to the ground.

"Like riding through the clouds," Lionel murmured dreamily. "Alas, the beauty of mist is transient, ephemeral, and cannot be captured by pen or brush."

"What's that?" The earl fixed his nephew with a nervous eye. "Wouldn't be going on prosing on like that if I was you, old fellow. People'll think you're short a sheet."

Lionel placed a hand on his heart. "You don't have an artist's soul, Uncle. Rosa—I mean, Miss Rosemary—would know what I mean."

Deering shook his head. Harcourt laughed and spurred Lancer forward, and he was in the lead when they rounded the loop in the road that led to the property of the late Sir Thomas Linden. This was no princely estate, but from this distance it had a spritely look to it with wide, fair paddocks, more than adequate stables, and a riding track that ran some distance from a comfortable brownstone dwelling.

"Sir Tom knew his horses," Deering commented. "Time was when he had no less than twenty blood horses here. Not ordinary cattle, mind. His animals raced at Newmarket. Had a cracking good jockey, name of Ableman, who won fat purses for him, give you m'word."

But it was soon obvious that this was all in the past. As he rode closer, Harcourt could see that the gardens were being choked with weeds. The roof of the house was in need of repair, and a broken window had been replaced by a sheet of wood. The chimney appeared ready to collapse at any given moment, and the courtyard was weedy.

But in this uninviting courtyard stood no less than five vehicles. There was a landau, three curricles, and a handsome perch phaeton drawn by smart-looking grays.

"B'dad," the earl exclaimed, "Lady Linden's got many callers, ain't she? Where's the confounded groom, though? He ought to be running to take our horses."

Harcourt glanced at the stable and noted that this was about the only passable spot in the whole estate. The sloping stable roof had been newly shingled, and its walls had been freshly whitewashed. Also, the riding track, though infested with weeds, gave evidence that someone had been trying to keep up appearances.

A procession of sorts was wending its way along this track. A tall, raw-boned man was plodding along in leading a neat pony. On the pony sat a small boy whose flushed face was almost eclipsed by a sailor hat that was too big for him. Following these individuals at some distance were Nella and two young boys mounted on geldings.

She was wearing a rusty black riding habit, and an old, thoroughly unfashionable bonnet perched on her head. But she carried herself with the grace and poise of a queen, and the stallion she was riding was magnificent. Proud, sleek and coal black, he walked as though he owned the earth.

Deering pursed his lips in a soundless whistle. "Thought all Sir Tom's cattle had been sold off after he died. Shows you, don't it, Court? Couldn't find a better animal than that black horse anyplace, give you my word."

Though a stallion was hardly the ideal mount for a lady, Nella was obviously equal to the challenge. She was moreover so absorbed in what she was doing that she did not notice that she had visitors.

"Simon," Harcourt heard her call as they drew nearer. "Remember to give your horse the central balance."

"B'dad," Deering exclaimed, enlightened. "She's giving those brats a riding lesson."

"Incline your body slightly forward," Nella continued. "Chest open, now, head up, and not so much weight on your buttocks."

Harcourt grinned appreciatively. If Lady Portwick could have heard *that*, she would have collapsed.

"No, do not pull, Lawrence," Nella warned. "No wonder your horse raises his nose up to the skies. He is not being wicked, he is only defending himself against pain from the snaffle bit. Imagine how you would dislike having someone hang on your mouth."

As she spoke, Nella became aware that she had an audience. She felt surprise not unmixed with anxiety as she saw the Earl of Deering, but she smiled when she saw the major and Lionel.

"How do you do!" she called. "Torfy?"

The big, raw-boned individual stopped in his

tracks, executed a slow turn, and whispered something unintelligible.

"Anselm has had enough riding for one day. Please to take him to the stables."

"But I don't *want* to go to the stables," the urchin with the big hat protested. "I want to continue riding, Miss Nella."

"I can see that, but your pony is fatigued," Nella smiled. "I am sure you would like to give him an apple. Torfy, please to give Anselm an apple after you have seen to the gentlemen's horses."

The big man mumbled what must be an agreement. "Torfy will see to your mounts, gentlemen," Nella continued. "If you will go to the house, my stepmother will make you welcome. And my sister, of course."

This last caused Lionel to blush. Deering gave Torfy a dubious look but began to trot his mount toward the house. "Coming, Court?"

As Harcourt turned to follow, a capricious gust of March wind blew along the riding track. It lifted the sailor's hat from the small boy's head and flung it almost directly at one of the older youth's horses. The gelding, astonished and frightened, reared up on its haunches and bolted.

Instinctively, Harcourt spurred after the boy on the runaway horse, but before he could reach the child, Nella swept by him. Her clear voice was calm and reassuring as she called, "Simon, remember what I taught you. Do not lose your head. Grip with your upper calves and knees and thighs."

As she spoke, she drew alongside the rampaging

gelding. Harcourt, who had come up on the other side, reached out to grasp the gelding's reins, but she shook her head. "Simon knows what to do."

Harcourt was not so sure. The child looked petrified with fear. Riding beside him, Nella continued her calm encouragement. "Good seat, Simon—you are doing magnificently. I am here, and Major Harcourt is beside you, so no harm can come to you. Show your horse that you are the master."

The stricken look began to leave the boy's face, and he followed Nella's instructions. As the horse was brought under control, Nella said, "Take him for one more turn, Simon, and then you and Lawrence may go to the stables and rub down your horses." She smiled and added warmly, "That was well done."

Simon's pale face flushed with pleasure. He grinned jauntily, and as he trotted his now subdued mount around the riding track, he held himself proudly erect.

"And well done to you, Miss Linden," Harcourt commented.

She looked up quickly to see the approval in his eyes. "Perhaps you think I was foolhardy, but Simon is a shy and timid boy and his mother cossets him too much. I wanted him to see what he could achieve if only he *dared*."

Excalibur shifted restively, and Nella controlled him almost absently. "Your stallion is very swift," Harcourt said. "Your sister is right. He's worth three of Saint Hugh the Brave."

Nella chuckled. "Best not to let Lady Portwick hear you say so."

Wind pulled at the brim of her drab bonnet, but Harcourt was not aware of its ugliness. He was thinking that he had never seen such a vivid face before. Under her twice-turned bonnet, Nella's cheeks were rosy, and her green eyes sparkled emerald in the sunlight.

"Are the lessons over for the day?" he asked.

She nodded. "The three boys you saw board their horses here, so Torfy is going to show them how to care for their mounts. I collect," she went on frankly, "that you have guessed that I take on riding students and board horses, too. They have helped to repair the stable."

"Then I wish you many more students."

His matter-of-fact reply erased the faint defensiveness that had crept into her voice. "I wish I could have more boarders because the house needs repairs. A shingle actually *fell* when Lord Moore came to call."

"Did it hit him?"

"No, but he looked very surprised and wondered if there had been an earthquake." Nella began to trot Excalibur toward the stable. "Angel was *mortified*."

Harcourt tried to remember who Lord Moore was and could not. "Your stepmother has several callers this morning," he hazarded.

"Besides Lord Moore there are Mr. Hampton and the Honorable Mr. Fairlie. Also the Honorable Percival Lake and his friend Mr. Battersea."

Mentally, Nella ran through these gentlemen's qualifications. Mr. Hampton was a widower in his forties but robust and the owner of land profitable in revenues. Messrs. Lake and Battersea were agreeable and pleasant but of little consequence financially. The Honorable Augustus Fairlie, alas, was a mere London fribble. He wore a jacket with padded shoulders that almost eclipsed his small head and spoke in an affected lisp. Lord Moore certainly had held the field thus far. But now that the Earl of Deering had arrived—

"Your stepmother made quite an impression at the ball last night," Harcourt was saying. "My friend is enraptured by her."

Nella frowned. "Oh," she said. "But he is—" She checked herself hastily and amended, "The earl has a certain reputation."

"Don't concern yourself. Deering is not half as black as he has been painted."

Nella said anxiously, "We heard that he fought a duel over a married lady. He is said to be mad with love for her."

"Deering, though the best of good fellows, falls in and out of love at an instant's notice. He's harmless, I assure you. As for Lady Linden, his attention will be to her advantage."

Nella watched a dry smile curl the major's fine lips. He seemed so worldly, so knowledgeable, that she felt countrified and young by comparison. "I do not understand," she faltered.

"If Deering is seen calling at Linden House, other gallants will follow his lead," Harcourt explained. "In polite circles it is good ton to have an earl as an admirer. Deering's example will encourage others to dance attendance on Lady Linden."

It made sense, of course, but at the same time his words gave Nella pause. What must the major think of the Lindens, she wondered. He knew that Sir Tom was a gambler. Her unwise comments last night had made it plain that his young widow was dangling after a rich husband. One of Sir Tom's daughters was a hoyden, the other a schemer—

Her plan had seemed so simple when she had first conceived it, but now it appeared crass and common. Suddenly, Nella could no longer bear to think of the poverty that had pushed poor Angel into the Marriage Mart. Impulsively she tapped her heel against Excalibur's side and urged him forward.

It was as though she had unleased lightning. Astounded, Harcourt watched the black stallion's burst of speed. His own horse was accounted fleet of foot, but Excalibur was lengths ahead even before Lancer had commenced to move.

Harcourt followed Nella as she bent low over her horse and flew about the weedy riding track, and the one thought in his mind was that he had seldom seen horse and rider so completely in sympathy. He followed her, urging Lancer to his greatest speed, but it was not nearly enough. When Nella finally slowed her steed, Harcourt was behind by several lengths.

He drew up alongside her and saluted. "To the victor, the spoils. Ma'am, you misnamed that horse. He should have been called Lightning."

She was a little embarrassed. "I am sorry, Major. I did not mean to bolt like that. It was just . . ." She paused and looked up at him in a wordless plea for understanding.

It was only a look, but in that infinitesimal second, Harcourt understood everything she wanted to say. He sensed her helplessness and frustration, her dislike for the course she had set her hand to, and her determination to see it through.

Without pausing to think, he reached out and covered her hand in its frayed glove. "You are magnificent," he told her.

Nella did not know what to do. The major was looking at her in a way that made her feel decidedly odd. Something was happening to her, and she did not understand it. Nella felt excited and exhilarated and a little frightened, and her heart had begun to thump in a tumultuous way. It was as though she were racing along on a horse too swift to control.

She looked up at him uncertainly and Harcourt, watching the sun dance on Nella Linden's face, saw also the shadows at the corners of her mouth. No one, Harcourt thought confusedly, had the right to have a mouth like that. Warm and generous and soft, it invited—no—*commanded* kissing.

Suddenly a scream shattered the silence.

"What in God's name was that?" the major exclaimed.

He was interrupted by another shriek that caused the air to vibrate like a tuning fork. "Oh, Lionel," Rosemary's piercing voice lamented. "Oh, this is a disaster. Won't someone help me? I do not know what to do."

# Chapter Five

With the swift reflexes of a soldier, Harcourt turned Lancer and began to gallop in the direction of the screams. Nella followed the major down a narrow path that led through what had been Lady Elizabeth's rose garden. There was no sign of Rosemary or Lionel anywhere.

Nella called, "Rosa, where are you?"

Rosemary now appeared from among the scraggly trees that bordered the rose garden. Clumps of moss and twigs adorned her brown walking-out dress, and her eyes looked wild. "Nella, help me—please help," she moaned.

Tumbling out of the saddle, Nella ran to her sister. "What is it? What has happened?"

"Lionel has fallen into the stinging nettles," Rosemary cried tragically.

Harcourt had also dismounted. He pushed a tree branch aside to disclose Lionel sitting in a patch of what appeared to be weeds. The youth's hat was off, his neckcloth awry, and he was struggling to get to his feet.

Harcourt strode over to Lionel. "Come, lad, take my hand."

"Stop!" Rosemary wailed. "You must not go in there, Major, or the nettles will sting you, too, and you will be covered with horrid little blisters. Oh, it is all my fault."

Nella grasped her sister by the shoulders and gave her an ungentle shake. "Stop shouting and tell us what happened. Why are you out here alone?"

Rosemary's hat had fallen off, and her brown mane of hair flew untidily in every direction. She looked ready to cry as she explained, "I wanted to sketch Lionel standing by those trees. It would have made such an interesting composition with the sunlight filtering through the leaves onto his hair."

"We were studying the effect of light," Lionel began, then yelped as the major pulled him free of the nettles. "Ow—It's my fault, Miss Linden. I tripped on a branch and fell into these filthy things."

"I should not have brought you here," the distressed Rosemary insisted. "Lionel, will you ever forgive me?"

Grasping Lionel by the shoulder, Harcourt began to hustle him back down the garden path. "We've got to neutralize as much of the poison as we can. Do you have dock leaves growing about here, Miss Linden?"

As distressed as she was, Nella recalled that once, when she had been stung by a nettle, Torfy had applied the juice of a certain leafy plant to her wound.

"I believe that they grow near to the stable," she said. "Torfy would know. I will take the horses there and ask him."

"Good. Bring me as many as you can. Let's go, lad—and you, too, Miss Rosa."

Taking hold of the horses' bridles, Nella hurried toward the stables. Rosemary's laments pursued her, and as she rounded the corner of the rose garden, she saw that Messrs. Lake and Battersea had run down the path to see what was going on. The others had gathered on the front steps. Angelica was looking pale and frightened but was being supported by Lord Moore on one side and by Deering on the other. Both of these gentlemen were eyeing the other askance. Hampton had grasped his cane and was holding it up as though to defend Angelica against all enemies while the Honorable Augustus Fairlie was looking very nervous and twittering, "What? What?" in a feeble voice.

"There is nothing to fear," Nella said as calmly as she could. "Mr. Canton has had a slight accident with some nettles." Then, spying Stubbs and Mrs. Brunce hovering in the background, she called, "Mrs. Brunce, Stubbs, please to assist Major Harcourt."

"Oh, dammo," Mrs. Brunce was heard to groan, but whatever else she said was lost as Major Harcourt appeared leading Lionel. Rosemary, trotting at his heels, had the look of a whipped puppy.

Nella hurried to take Excalibur and Lancer to the stable and to consult Torfy, who led her to a patch of dock leaves. "Ay, they're the best remedy for nettle stings that I know of," he whispered as he helped her gather the leafy stems. "That major knows what he's doing."

She hurried back to the house with her harvest and was informed that the major had closeted himself upstairs in Sir Tom's rooms with Lionel. She sent Stubbs up with the dock leaves, then turned to announce to the others that the crisis was over. "Torfy assures me that the major knows what he is doing," she concluded, "so there is nothing to fear."

A tortured howl wafted downstairs. Rosemary covered her face with her hands, and Lord Moore, looking scandalized, said, "One is extremely sorry for young Canton. However, one wonders how he happened to come near such noxious weeds as nettles."

He bent a repressive look upon Rosemary, who stammered, "We were sk-sketching."

Lord Moore's thin, dark eyebrows shot up, and he sniffed. "Indeed," he murmured.

Though thoroughly exasperated at Rosemary's harebrained behavior, Nella felt sorry for her sister. "Fortunately," she said, "nettles will not do any lasting damage."

"It buwns, though," twittered the Honorable Augustus Fairlie. "Buwns like a wasp's sting, don't you know. Wouldn't want to be in Canton's shoes, 'pon wep." He shuddered as another yell wafted down the stairs and added, "Forgive me for weaving you, Wady Winden, but I can't bear sounds of pain. Hope you don't think me hen heawted."

Mr. Hampton soon followed the London dandy out the door. As Mr. Lake and his friend likewise took their leave, Lord Moore finally rose to his feet.

"If one may, one would beg to call upon you at a more suitable time, Lady Linden," he proclaimed. He then bent over Angelica's hand, shot a censorious look at the dejected Rosemary, bowed stiffly to Nella and Deering, and departed.

"Stiff-rumped stick," the earl muttered.

Nella frowned at him. She wished that Deering would offer to assist the major. Instead, he drew up a settee near Angelica and sat down on it.

"Don't worry about that young cub, Lady Linden," he said in a caressing voice. "Clumsy, y'know. Falls over his own feet all the time. Born like that."

"But to fall into nettles," Angelica protested, "and on our property, too. I thought that Torfy burned them out last autumn."

"They must have grown back." Nella glanced at Rosemary, who was sitting disconsolately near the doorway of the morning room. Her guileless brown eyes were enormous with remorse. Whenever she sighed, which was often, the weeds sticking to her hair trembled.

Nella would have liked to take her sister upstairs so that she could change her clothes and tidy herself, but she did not dare to leave the earl alone with Angelica. She frowned at his lordship, who had so forgotten propriety as to take Angelica's hand.

"My lord earl," she said sternly, "should you not be helping Major Harcourt?"

The earl looked astonished. "B'dad, ma'am, it'd be like carrying coals to Newcastle. Court can do anything."

"The major is being very kind." Angelica was not certain that she should allow the earl to hold her hand, but she did not wish to hurt his feelings. He had such beautiful eyes, as clear a blue as a summer sky. Besides, Angelica told herself, Nella and Rosemary were both in the room.

"Court's an excellent fellow," the earl agreed. "Saved m'life on the Peninsula. Would have died, give you my word, if he hadn't seen m'horse throw me. Stood over me and killed a dozen Frenchies—cut 'em down as if they'd been made of butter. Carried me back to our lines. Brave man, Court, and a true friend. None better, b'dad."

Angelica paled. "You were wounded, my lord?"

The earl pressed the white hand he held. "Don't let it give you the slightest concern."

His voice was soft. It held a practiced caress. Nella cleared her throat loudly and said, "Sir, I think that you *must* see how your nephew does."

With the greatest reluctance, Deering rose to his feet. Just then, however, there was the sound of a door opening, and the major's voice was heard calling for Stubbs. "We've got to get you home now, lad," he added.

Rosemary jumped to her feet and ran into the hall. Next moment, she wailed in dismay. Nella, who had followed her sister into the hall, bit back a wholly inappropriate desire to laugh as Lionel came down the stairs. Since his clothes were covered with nettles, Mrs. Brunce had supplied Lionel with some of the late Sir Tom's garments. Sir Tom had been at least twice Lionel's girth and several inches shorter, and the youth resembled a scarecrow.

Rosemary began to sniffle. Lionel was too embarassed to say anything to her, but as Harcourt passed her by, he paused for a moment. "Don't take it to heart, Miss Rosa," he told her. "It was an accident and not your fault. Besides, it'd take more than a few weeds to do a man harm."

Now that, Nella thought, was kind of the major. She was further cheered by the determined way in which he added, "We'll be on our way now. Deering, take the lad's arm. Servant, Lady Linden. Miss Linden, Miss Rosa, your most obedient."

As he swept his friend and Lionel out the door that Stubbs held open, Nella drew a heartfelt sigh. "Thank heavens," she exclaimed.

"You mean, 'thank heavens for the major,' " Mrs. Brunce corrected. "Nettles, is it? I cannot tell you what the world is coming to, indeed to God. Miss Rosa, stop your crying and tell us what you were thinking of, going off alone with young Mr. Canton?"

Rosemary blew her nose. "It was terribly boring in the house. Lord Moore and the earl were either making sheep's eyes at Angel or glaring at each other, and Mr. Hampton was prosing on about the price of wool, and that horrible little Fairlie creature was preening and tittering and lisping till I could have drowned him."

"But to go off without a chaperon," Mrs. Brunce persisted. "*Ach y fy*, Miss Rosa. I brought you up better than that."

"Well, what about Nella?" Rosemary retorted indignantly. "She was riding whoops about the track with Major Harcourt."

"We were not—" Nella began, then remembered

not only that impromptu race but the inexplicable feelings she had experienced.

If Rosa had not screamed when she did, what might have happened? The question made Nella uncomfortable enough to be cross. "Rosa," she said sharply, "do go upstairs and change out of that horrible dress. You look like Ophelia! And we need not stand about as if someone has just died. Mrs. Brunce, perhaps you will make us some tea."

"Tea!" The tears that had been trembling in Rosemary's eyes vanished as though by magic. She jumped to her feet, shedding twigs and moss and weeds, and cried, "What a famous thought. Cut the bread thick, Bruncie, won't you? I vow that anxiety has made me horribly hungry."

Next morning as they sat down to breakfast in the chilly morning room, Angelica suggested that they pay a call on the Portwicks. "It would only show proper feeling if we were to inquire after poor Mr. Canton," she said. "Do you not think so, dearest?"

Engaged in trying to warm her hands by clasping them about her teacup, Nella hesitated. "Normally, I would agree with you," she said, "but Lady Portwick will not be happy to see us. She has never liked us, and after what has happened to Lionel, she is certain to loathe us."

"But if we do not call, we will appear rude," Angelica pointed out.

"Who is being rude?" Rosemary wanted to know. Nella noted that her younger sister's eyes were glowing with purpose as she added, "Did I hear Angel say that we must go and see Lionel? I think it is a famous idea. I am dressed for it, see?"

Throwing out her hands, she spun about on her toes and nearly sent the teacups crashing to the floor. As she rescued the crockery, Nella noted that Rosemary had put on her best walking-out dress of amber muslin. It had been turned only twice, and a band of lace disguised the spots of paint that would not come clean in the wash. With the color in her cheeks and the eagerness in her eyes, Rosemary looked quite pretty.

Angelica smiled at her older stepdaughter. "Well, dearest, what do you say now?"

It did not take the Linden ladies hours to dress. They had little to choose from in the way of costume, and their serviceable bonnets covered hair that had been arranged quite simply. Within an hour of having breakfast, Torfy had hitched old Rumtum up to the family's battered old barouche.

This vehicle had not been sold with the other conveyances because no one would bid for it. In spite of all of Torfy's efforts at mending and patching together, the upholstery sagged and the left wheel had a distressing way of listing to one side. The barouche squeaked and creaked as the ladies mounted, and Nella warned, "If Lady Portwick does not receive us, do not be surprised. We may have to turn around with nothing accomplished."

"Pooh," Rosemary said cheerfully. "Even if she does not see us, Lionel will know we came to ask about him. Besides, Nella, it is a beautiful day for a drive in the country."

Indeed, the day was warm for March and blessed with scattered sunlight. As they trundled the road toward Portwick Hall, Rosemary began an old Welsh song that Mrs. Brunce had taught them, Nella joined in, and Angelica hummed along. By the time they had reached the great Portwick gates, all three were cheerful and ready even for an encounter with Lady Portwick.

Ignoring the astonished looks bent on them by the gatekeeper and the groom who came to hold Rumtum's head, Nella gave her name to the glacial-eyed butler who met them on the ground-floor anteroom and asked if her ladyship was home to visitors. The butler bowed and said that he would see.

Leaving the ladies in the hall, he walked haughtily away. In a few moments, a door opened on the first floor and they could clearly hear Lady Portwick's voice. They could not hear what was said, but it was clear that she was not overjoyed.

"I warned you," Nella was pointing out when the door opened and the Earl of Deering came running down the stairs.

"Lady Linden," he exclaimed. "Kind of you to call. Good of you, b'dad."

Bending over Angelica's hand, he turned a happy smile to her companions. "Your most obedient, ladies. M'sister is eager to welcome you. Waiting anxiously in the yellow drawing room, give you m'word."

Offering his arm to Angelica, he led the way up the stairs. Rosemary tipped a broad wink at Nella as the sisters followed through the carpeted foyer into a room decorated in shades of gold and yellow. Saffron curtains screened the tall, many-paned windows, a yellow and beige carpet embraced the floor, and the upholstery of various overstuffed chairs ranged from hues of strawberry gold to orange.

Lady Portwick was enthroned on a Chinese daybed. Its bright yellow hue gave her a slightly jaundiced look, and the expression in her eyes was decidedly unfriendly as she spoke through closed teeth. "Lady Linden."

Ignoring the lady's tone, Angelica and her stepdaughters made their curtseys. "I hope that we do not intrude," Angelica said diffidently. "We were so concerned about Mr. Canton. How is he this morning?"

"Lionel," Lady Portwick said in a repressive voice, "had a most uncomfortable night." Her glare added clearly, Thanks to you. "He is resting."

"No, he ain't," her brother promptly corrected. "The halfling's outside in the garden. Court took him."

Lady Portwick's generous bosom swelled. "Major Harcourt took my son *outside*? Why was I not told? Deering, ring for Yates at once."

"Oh, stubble it, Maria," Deering advised impatiently. "Lad's not at death's door. A few pimples ain't going to kill him." He turned to Angelica, adding solicitously, "Sofa is comfortable, ma'am. Will you ladies be seated? I'll fetch the brat."

A dreadful silence descended in the room as the earl whistled himself out. As though she could not bear to even look upon her unwelcome guests, Lady Portwick glared into space. Rosemary fidgeted,

Angelica bit her lip. Nella, who had expected Turkish treatment, peaceably remarked, "It is a lovely day."

In quelling tones Lady Portwick replied, "It will rain."

"Oh, surely not," Rosemary exclaimed, alarmed. "I hope you are wrong, ma'am. I intend to sketch all day, you see." She saw that she had blundered and made things worse by adding, "But of course you aren't interested in things like that. Lionel told me."

The impertinent hussy dared to call her son by his given name! But before Lady Portwick could give vent to her displeasure, there were footsteps on the stairs. Deering, followed by Lionel, came in.

"Miss Rosa," Lionel exclaimed.

Completely forgetting that there were others in the room, he walked over to her and shook hands. "How good of you to come and see me," he cried.

Ignoring Lady Portwick's hiss of disapproval, Rosemary replied cordially, "I wanted to see if you were covered with pimples. I am relieved to see that you are not. The dock leaves have done their work well."

"Major Harcourt's doing," Lionel began, when Lady Portwick interrupted.

"Why," she demanded sternly, "were you outside, Lionel? Did I not expressly enjoin you to remain in bed?"

The happy expression disappeared from Lionel's eyes. He flushed and muttered, "I was g-getting some air, Mama."

"Air is what you should expressly avoid," his mother lectured. "After the shock you received yesterday, you must not be subjected to cold air."

"You are right as always, ma'am." Harcourt had sauntered in on the heels of her ladyship's lecture and stood smiling at her. "Cold air won't help Lionel, but the warmth of the sun works wonders. Your knowledge continues to amaze me."

Nella had always supposed the major to be a brave man. Now she was sure of it. She watched admiringly as Harcourt met Lady Portwick's wrathful gaze, then casually dismissed her and turned to bow to her unwelcome guests.

He then smiled down at Nella and said, "Did you ride Excalibur over to Portwick Hall, Miss Linden?"

"No, for he'll not abide being placed in the shafts. Rumtum did the honors," she replied.

"Ah. Then you were quite safe."

Even though he appeared grave, his eyes were smiling. "Perfectly, since there were no curricles on the road," Nella agreed.

No one asked her what she meant. In fact, no one was paying them the slightest attention. Deering was eagerly talking to Angelica, Lady Portwick was tongue-lashing Lionel and Rosemary was watching them unhappily.

It was too bad, Nella thought, that Lionel did not have Major Harcourt's courage. "Your remedies yesterday were effective, Major," she said aloud. "Lionel seems to have taken no hurt. How did you know what to do?"

"Knowledge from a misspent youth in the country" was the easy reply.

"Did you spend that youth here in Hampshire?" Nella asked.

"Much of it, yes."

His lips were smiling, but his eyes were not. Nella could now understand why Lady Portwick gave ground to the major. Few would enjoy crossing a man who could look as he did now.

Then he smiled, and the hardness in his eyes went away. "Your sister seems to have recovered from her adventures."

"It is impossible to repress Rosa for long. She was only a baby when Mama died, and though Mrs. Brunce tried her best, she picked up a great many of Sir Tom's free and easy ways." Nella sent her sister a fond but exasperated look. "Rosa is what you would call 'an original.' She speaks her mind before she thinks, and she does as she pleases. If we had a fortune, she would be called eccentric. Alas, as it is, people laugh at her."

The butler now entered the room with a silver tray. On it were a decanter of sherry for the gentlemen, ratafia and lemonade for the ladies, and a plate of delicate comfitures made of sugar. Nella saw Rosemary's eyes glisten at the sight of those delectable treats and wished she were closer by so as to give her a warning nudge.

Lady Portwick waved the refreshments away, and Angelica also declined, but when the butler offered Rosemary his tray, she picked up several of the comfitures and popped two into her mouth.

"How excellent," she exclaimed in carrying tones. "What a pity we cannot afford to have such delicious things at home."

All conversation stopped. Lady Portwick suggested, "In that case you had better have another bonbon, miss. In fact, why not take several?"

Sarcasm was wasted on Rosemary, who took a handful of sweets. The butler looked pained. Angelica reddened. Lionel looked embarrassed.

Nella was mortified. "Oh, Rosa," she whispered, "no."

Rosemary looked around her and realized that she had committed yet another social gaffe. She looked at the comfitures in her hand and then at the floor. The healthy glow of her cheeks turned into a mortified crimson.

"Perhaps," Lady Portwick said in a poisonously sweet voice, "you have eaten too many sweets, Miss Linden. You look all abroad."

Nella threw up her head at this, but before she could come to her sister's defense, Harcourt was strolling across the room. He helped himself to one of the confections and smiled at Rosemary.

"You're right, Miss Rosemary, they *are* very good," he said. Then, picking up the silver tray that the butler had laid down, he turned to Nella. "May I tempt you?"

The look in his gray eyes told Nella that he was as angry as she was. In a clear voice she replied, "You may, indeed."

Calmly, the major went about the room, offering his comfitures. Deering took one. Angelica followed suit. Frowning, Lady Portwick shook her head, but Harcourt remained standing before her.

"There is a custom in the east," he said in his smooth way, "wherein a hostess always breaks bread with her guests. Not to do so is considered bad manners."

Lady Portwick opened her mouth to tell the major that she had no intention of taking a bonbon and encountered a look so cold and hard that it astonished her. In spite of herself, she felt her hand reaching for the tray.

"Well, perhaps one," Lady Portwick gritted.

Nella watched Lady Portwick eating sugar as though it were acid. She felt idiotically happy. It was as though Harcourt's championship had wiped away all unpleasantness in the room. The conversation began again, and Lionel actually plucked up the courage to walk away from his mother's side and sit down by Rosemary. The earl was right, Nella thought. Major Harcourt was a man who could carry anything off.

Nevertheless, she knew that they must leave at once. Though cowed for the moment, Lady Portwick would soon rally. Nella looked meaningfully at Angelica, but her stepmother was not attending. She was listening to the earl say, "But you would be safe in my hands, m'lady. Court, convince Lady Linden that she'd be safe with me."

"What is this?" Nella wondered aloud.

"The earl has asked me to ride out with him tomorrow in his carriage," Angelica explained.

Nella was taken aback. When had all this come

about? She listened attentively as the earl exclaimed, "Just the thing, give you my word. Short ride in the country—take the spring air—beg you'll agree to go, Lady Linden. You'll come to no harm with me."

Lady Portwick sniffed. "Deering, what can you be thinking of? Lady Linden is just out of mourning. It is unseemly for her to be seen racketing about with you—"

"—without a chaperon. Quite so," Harcourt interrupted smoothly. "I agree with you, ma'am."

Deering looked gratefully at his friend. "Then you and Miss Linden will come with us, Court? B'dad, Miss Linden, you could show off that handsome black stallion."

Angelica's lovely amethyst eyes were bright with pleasure. "I vow that it would be greatly entertaining. Do you not think so, dearest?"

Nella thought of what Major Harcourt had told her yesterday. If Angelica was seen in Deering's company, her consequence would no doubt be greatly enhanced. Eligible gentlemen would realize it was fashionable to flock about the lovely young widow.

And yet, there was Deering. Nella did not trust the earl for a moment. He was charming and handsome, and already he had made an impression on Angel.

From across the room, Harcourt watched his friend. Deering's handsome face was flushed with pleasure, and his eyes held a look that was all too familiar. The sapskull had fallen in love once again.

Good-bye Lady Barbara, he thought. Then, when

he saw how worried Nella looked, his cynicism faded.

"Well, Court," Deering was urging. "What about it? A guinea says that Lancer can't beat the lady's black stallion."

"Done. But Miss Linden may choose to ignore the challenge."

The weather had been good of late. Excalibur yearned for real exercise, and so did she. Surely, Nella thought, she and the major could between them make sure that the earl behaved himself.

"Nella?" Angelica asked hopefully, "will you?"

Angelica had been so good, so willing. She deserved her outing. Nella smiled at her stepmother, then looked up to meet the major's steady gray eyes.

"Why not?" she said.

# Chapter Six

During the return journey to Linden House, the occupants of the ancient barouche each pursued her own thoughts. Rosemary was scowling, but a soft smile curved Angelica's lips. Seeing that smile, Nella was disturbed.

"Angel," she warned, "it would not be wise to fall in love with the Earl of Deering."

"I do not intend to do anything of the kind," Angelica replied dreamily.

Her cheeks grew pink, her eyes luminous, and Nella's concern became real anxiety. She began to regret tomorrow's outing. Pitting her inexperienced young stepmother against a seasoned London rake seemed now to be great folly.

"Are you sure?" she prodded gently. "Deering is handsome and has much charm, but collect that he was involved in a scandal before he left London."

"We do not know if what we heard is true," Angelica protested. "You always say you dislike people who gossip, Nella."

"Unfortunately, where there is smoke there is usually fire." Nella hesitated for a moment before adding, "There is something else. Deering is a peer, and when he takes a wife, he will most probably marry a social equal."

Angelica took Nella's hand. "Do not be concerned that I am setting my cap for Deering. I am simply playing the marriage game, and flirting is one of the rules."

Nella looked at the small, gloved hand and wondered whether she was overreacting. Angelica was young and looked vulnerable, but she had also been on the Marriage Mart before. No doubt her odious family had made sure that she had learned all the rules of the game.

She smiled and said, "In that case, an outing may do us both good."

"Besides, it enraged Lady Portwick," the irrepressible Rosemary added. "She is ruining poor Lionel's life. She is what Sir Tom would have called a female Captain Hackum."

Privately, Nella thought that Lionel lacked spirit. He had not come to Rosemary's defense today, and if Major Harcourt had not risen to the occasion, Lady Portwick's rudeness would have gone unchecked.

Rosemary went on, "I am glad Lionel has a friend like Major Harcourt. Depend upon it, the major would not allow Lady Portwick to rake coals over *his* head. Besides, I like the way he laughs with his eyes."

But those gray eyes could also become hard and cynical. Nella reminded herself that Harcourt had saved the earl's life in battle and could make someone like Lady Portwick toe the mark. And, behind those smiling eyes that Rosemary admired, there were secrets.

"I wonder what they are," she murmured.

The ladies were again silent, lost in their private thoughts. Rumtum plodded along, snuffling with relief and anticipation as they turned the loop in the road that led to Linden House. As the house itself came into view, Nella saw that they had visitors.

"Is that Lord Moore?" she asked. But instead of his lordship's perch phaeton, a landau stood by the stable door, and as they rattled into the courtyard, they could hear Torfy shouting.

"Tha cannot coom in here," he was yelling. "Get thee gone, othergates I'll make thee go."

Nella exchanged startled glances with her stepmother, and Rosemary exclaimed incredulously, "That can't be *Torfy* bellowing."

As she spoke, a man in a fashionable dove-gray riding cape, beaver hat, and polished boots came hurriedly backing out of the stable. He was closely followed by Torfy, who held a pitchfork aimed at the stranger's portly midsection.

"Damn your impudence," the gentleman spluttered. "You'll pay for this."

"Nay, I asked thee polite first," Torfy roared. "Happen this is all tha can understand."

Nella called sharply, "What is going on here?"

Both men turned. Torfy, looking relieved, exclaimed, "Eh, Miss Nella, this mawworm pushed his way into the stable."

"The idiot is lying," the other snarled.

Nella's eyes had gone as cold as jadestone. In a frosty voice she demanded, "What are you doing here, Mr. Purvis?"

The man seemed to make an effort to control his temper. Removing the curly beaver from his head, he bowed so deeply that his polished boots creaked. "Ladies, your most obedient," he drawled. "I'm here for a friendly visit."

His red-cheeked, chinless face sagged into a smile that Nella did not return. "You are not welcome here. Please to leave at once."

Torfy gestured with his pitchfork, and the smile slid from Purvis's face. "High in the instep, Miss Linden?" he sneered. "Maybe you'd better have a look at this."

He put a hand into his cloak pocket and withdrew a paper. "I think you'll recognize the signature."

Nella's heart had begun to sink even before Purvis held the paper up for her inspection. She didn't need to see the familiar, scrawled signature to know that she was looking at another of Sir Tom's gambling notes.

"How much?" she asked wearily.

Purvis neighed with laughter. "You're as quick as a flea's leap, I'll give you that. I always told Sir Tom that you should have been a man, Miss Nella."

Nella wished that she *were* a man and could give Purvis the hiding he deserved. She hated the familiar way he used her first name, and she loathed the man himself. Purvis was one of the horse fanciers who haunted the Newmarket track, and the reputation of underhanded dealing clung to him like a foul mist. The Jockey Club regarded him with suspicion, but so far nothing could be proven against him, for Purvis was clever.

But it was his cruelty that enraged Nella. Many were the fine young horses that Purvis had bought, trained, and raced mercilessly until they dropped. And if this were not enough to damn the man, he victimized his own kind as well. Purvis was known to prey on gentlemen who had sustained heavy losses at Newmarket. More than once Nella had watched Purvis sidle up to some ashen-faced young blood after a race, offer the loan of money, and get his note. At a later date, he would come to collect collateral that was ten times the value of the loan.

As he had come to collect now. He was saying, "Sir Tom was badly dipped when he came to me. I'm no talepitcher, mind, but the man was at point non plus. I offered him a loan out of friendship—"

"On what collateral?" Nella interrupted tersely.

Purvis cocked back his shoulders and rocked back and forth on his boot heels. "You've got a black stallion named Excalibur," he began.

The man wanted Excalibur. All the blood in Nella's body seemed to have turned to ice, there was a roaring in her ears, and she felt sick and dizzied. From far away she could hear Rosemary saying heatedly, "You can't have Excalibur. Go away, you horrid little beast."

Purvis was enjoying himself. "Why blame me? It was your papa's fault for putting rolls of soft he didn't have on splay-footed, herring-gutted, cow-hocked windsucker."

Nella's dizziness disappeared as though by magic. Seizing her whip, she struck at Purvis. The blow knocked off his hat, which landed in the mud.

"Get out!" Nella shouted.

"Why, you little vixen!" As Purvis attempted to catch Nella's whip hand, she hit him again. This blow caught his outstretched hand, and he yelled in pain.

Stammering with rage, he bellowed, "I have your precious father's note, and I own that black beast of yours. Put down that whip, you hellcat, or I'll make you sorry."

Nella jumped down from the barouche and flew after Purvis. She did not waste her energy in words but struck at him with all the force of her arm. The man yelped as one blow caught him on the back, another on his shoulder. He turned and caught another blow full in the face.

"Damn you," he roared, "I'll teach you—"

"Tha'll teach nowt to nobody." Torfy ranged himself at Nella's side. Waving his pitchfork threateningly, he added, "Sneck up and leave now or get a bang on the lug."

Rosemary scrambled into the driver's seat and urged Rumtum forward. "You knocker-faced rail, I will ride you down," she shouted, and Angelica cried, "Get off our land, you—you villain!"

In the face of this united front, Purvis turned tail and made for his landau. He scrambled up into the driver's seat and then spat over the side. "I'll be back," he threatened.

"He will," Torfy muttered. "Is it true as our Excalibur belongs to yon clodhead, Miss Nella?"

The fight had drained out of Nella. She felt physically sick as she watched Purvis's landau disappearing down the road. "I am afraid so," she replied.

She turned to look at Angelica, and their eyes met in mutual realization. Time was running out for the Lindens. If they did not act at once, it would be too late. But before she could put this thought into words, Rosemary groaned.

"Is it not the outside of enough?" Rosemary complained. "Here comes that tiresome Lord Moore."

Nella came to life with a jerk. "Angel, go into the house and smooth your hair. Rosa, tell Mrs. Brunce to make tea. Torfy, take charge of Rumtum. Hurry! We must make a good impression on his lordship."

Accordingly, when Lord Moore knocked on the front door some few minutes later, he was met by Stubbs, who greeted him as though he were royalty and ushered him into a morning room. Here he was received by the Linden sisters and a pale but determined Angelica.

"It was good of you to come," she murmured, as Lord Moore bent over her hand. "We are so dull here of an afternoon. Your company is welcome, my lord."

Lord Moore was gratified. Though Lady Linden had seemed cordial enough yesterday, he noted that the rackety Earl of Deering had commanded most of her attention. Now, however, the enchanting young widow hung on every word he uttered.

Nor did her stepdaughters do anything to disturb

the peace. Rosemary looked unusually subdued today and did not shock him with her hoydenish ways. Nella served tea and an excellent cake and prevailed upon Lady Linden to play on the spinet. When she obediently sat down at the instrument and played a sentimental love song, Lord Moore felt positively complacent. He was now sure that the fair Angelica had conceived a *tendre* for him.

Even when other callers arrived—the pimply Augustus Fairlie and several other and more serious rivals for the lady's attention—Lord Moore felt as though he still was the primary focus of Lady Linden's regard. He accordingly stayed longer than polite convention allowed and actually outlasted all the other callers. When he finally kissed Lady Linden's hand good-bye, he did so with regret.

"One has seldom enjoyed such fair company," he said meaningfully. "One hopes to see your ladyship again, soon."

Angelica's reply fanned the hopes in Lord Moore's narrow chest. It was well for him that he did not observe Nella sagging against the door after she had seen him through it, or hear Rosemary's explosive, "Thank heavens *that* is over. I feel as if I have been sitting on a pincushion all afternoon."

"You behaved most beautifully," Nella approved. "And Lord Moore is quite pleasant company. Do you not think so, Angel?"

Angelica nodded without much enthusiasm. "I suppose so. Only, he is so serious, and he makes me feel like a flutterhead."

"He looks at *me* as if I were a black beetle,"

Rosemary sniffed. "I am glad that he is not *my* suitor, I can tell you. The man is a forty-jawed bore. All afternoon he has spoken of nothing but his land in Hampshire and his country estate in Sussex and his house in London."

"All of which mean that his lordship is rich," Nella pointed out firmly.

Angelica got to her feet. "I have the headache and am going to my room. Do not be concerned about me, dearest. I am only a little tired."

It could not be helped, Nella told herself miserably as she watched Angelica climb the stairs. Lord Moore was a trifle serious, perhaps, and she could not but dislike the censorious or shocked look in his eyes when Rosemary did or said something out of the way. Even so, he was the pick of the suitors.

If only the man was not so *slow*. Lord Moore was nothing if not a methodical man. His character was such that he would not do anything or say anything on impulse. By his own admission, it had taken him a whole year to find the exact perch phaeton that suited him. He weighed things, looked at every argument from every corner, researched every move. He would never offer for a lady without courting her for several years.

The Lindens did not have the luxury of several years or even weeks. Nella was now glad that she had agreed to ride out with the earl and Major Harcourt tomorrow. Perhaps hearing that Angelica had been seen riding in the earl's carriage would spur Lord Moore to declare himself before Purvis got his claws on Excalibur.

* * *

Nella slept fitfully that night. It had started to rain before she went to bed, and she was afraid that the bad weather would continue and ruin the plans for the next day. But a brisk March wind blew in toward dawn and scattered the rain clouds, so that when Nella rose to look out at the brightening east, she saw the rim of the sun peering over the horizon.

"A good omen," she murmured.

As though to prove her right, the day dawned clear and bright, and Torfy sent word that Excalibur was in fine fettle. It was Stubbs who delivered this message to the breakfast table, but Mrs. Brunce supplied the details.

"And as usual," she said disparagingly, "that Torfy wouldn't lift his voice over a whisper or look me in the eye. A mouse you have got there instead of a groom."

"You would not have thought so if you had seen him pointing his pitchfork at that muffin-faced Purvis," Rosemary said. "Torfy was like a knight of old, Bruncie."

A glint of interest flashed in the Welshwoman's eyes, but it was hastily suppressed. "Get along with you, Miss Rosa. Talking nonsense you are, with the earl arriving in only a little moment."

As it turned out, it lacked half an hour to the appointed time when the earl appeared driving his curricle. Deering himself leaped down to knock on the door, and his voice was eager as he asked Stubbs to inform Lady Linden that he awaited her pleasure.

Mounted on his bay stallion, Harcourt was both amused and surprised. He had half expected his indolent friend to be abed until the last moment, but Deering had risen early and had hardly stopped to breakfast in his impatience to be gone. He had been short with his sister, had barely tolerated the jocose comments of his bleary-eyed brother-in-law, and had snapped at Lionel to stop acting like a mooncalf and put some pepper under his tail.

Plainly, Deering was in love again. It was, Harcourt considered, just as well that their stay in Hampshire would not be for too much longer, or he would be once again making a fool of himself.

Just then he saw Nella leading her coal-black stallion out of the stable. Today she was dressed in a moss-green riding dress and a riding hat of the same material. It was not of the latest style, Harcourt's knowledgeable eye told him, but a sweep of bronze feathers gave it dash.

He dismounted and strolled over to greet her and noted that, though she smiled as he shook her hand, Nella's eyes were bleak.

She was in some kind of difficulty. He was sure of that much, but this was not the time or place for questions. Instead, Harcourt watched Nella as she greeted Deering and then turned to mount her own horse.

"May I assist you?" Harcourt asked.

Nella was thinking of Lord Moore as she placed her hand in the major's, but then all thoughts of his stodgy lordship fled. Major Harcourt's grip was firm, and he lifted her so effortlessly. For a heartbeat's time he held her close against his hard body, and she had a confused impression of searching gray eyes under wind-ruffled hair that had the look of crisp, dark silk.

Nella was suddenly seized by the idiotish desire to run her ungloved fingers through that silk. She felt the almost ungovernable need to let those same fingers trace the tanned line of his cheek and to caress the faint, moon-shaped scar near his temple. Her heart was racing as she settled herself into her saddle and gathered up Excalibur's reins.

The party got under way at once. Followed by Rosemary's yodels of farewell, Deering drove sedately out the gate and onto the road. Nella followed closely, and Harcourt kept pace with her, thinking that she was looking pale. It was as though the sun had retreated behind a cloud. He held his peace until the carriage had found the open road and then asked, "Are you still concerned that Deering is being too attentive to your stepmother?"

"No," she replied, "you were right. Being seen in the earl's company will increase her consequence."

As she spoke, they turned a corner in the road and encountered the Honorable Augustus Fairlie. That gentleman was dressed in a blue coat with enormous buttons, buff pantaloons, and a shirt collar that rose so steeply behind his head that he looked deformed. He was obviously on his way to call at Linden House, and the haste with which he whipped out his quizzing glass was comical.

Harcourt observed idly, "That fribble is sure to broadcast it around Hampshire that Deering and Lady Linden were driving out together."

"I hope so," Nella exclaimed.

Her vehemence made Harcourt raise a quizzical eyebrow. "Something is bothering you," he said frankly. "Is there some way I can be of service to you?"

Nella had promised herself that she would not tell anyone about Purvis's visit, but now she could not keep back the words. "Yesterday when we returned—" she began, and then checked herself. "It is nothing."

Harcourt watched the way she gripped the reins as she spoke and noted the shake in her usually steady hand as she stroked her horse's ebony neck. "Something to do with Excalibur," he hazarded.

*"How did you know?"*

"A guess. What happened when you returned home yesterday?" Harcourt prompted.

He sounded so calm and sure of himself. He had been in the war, he knew the world, and perhaps he could advise her. But when Nella had told him about Purvis's threat, his reaction was not the one she expected.

"You say the fellow dared threaten you?"

His voice was one that Nella had not heard from him before. His eyes had gone stone hard, his mouth had narrowed to a white line. "The blackguard should be horsewhipped," Major Harcourt gritted.

"He was," Nella pointed out.

Eyes that were almost black with anger swung toward her. "I can understand why you went after him, but it was foolish. A bas—a villain like that wouldn't hesitate to attack a woman. By God, I wish I'd been there."

On the point of saying more, Harcourt checked himself. He realized that Nella was staring at him in astonishment. He could scarcely blame her, for he himself was surprised at the raw rage that was boiling inside him. If he had been there when Purvis threatened Nella, he would have broken his neck.

Suddenly, Harcourt was confused. This protectiveness was not only foreign to him but completely inappropriate. He had no right to protect Nella Linden, no *interest* in protecting her. He had seen her twice before this—three times, if he counted their unorthodox first meeting. By rights he should not have given her more than a passing thought.

Instead of which he had been thinking of her a great deal. Until now, he had explained away his interest in the unconventional Linden Family by rationalizing that he was bored with the Portwicks. But mere boredom could not explain the murderous fury that still seethed through him.

With an effort of will that was almost physically painful, Harcourt forced himself to remain calm. He had been in Hampshire too long. He had been in *England* too long. Suddenly, he longed for the simplicity of battle, for decisions about life and death that were far safer than a woman's green eyes.

In a low voice Nella was saying, "Pray do not be troubled. Purvis is our problem, not yours, and we must solve it in our own way."

True, Harcourt thought. Aloud he said, "I hope that you will find the means to do so."

Preoccupied by her problems, Nella did not note

the uncharacteristic formality with which he spoke. "The *means* is Lord Moore. To give you words without any bark on them, he is a man of property and wealth. He has been dancing attendance on Angel. If he offers for her, our creditors will see that she is making an excellent match and extend us credit."

"Good thinking," Harcourt approved. "Love in a cottage does not last long, Miss Linden."

He sounded so definite that she glanced at him questioningly and saw that a dry smile curled his lip. "My parents tried it, to their sorrow."

Nella was too taken aback to say anything.

"My father," Harcourt continued in a calm, deliberate voice, "was a marquis's son. He was a viscount's nephew. I am told that his family owned a great deal of land in Scotland as well as here in England. He was a second son, but he would have been a wealthy man had he not fallen in love with my mother. She was the very beautiful, very accomplished daughter of a penniless country curate. When they married, they did so without the family's blessing. My father was disinherited, and his family never spoke to him or saw him again."

Instinct told Nella that Harcourt had never spoken of this matter before. He chose his words with a care that spoke of hidden pain as, with studied nonchalance, he spoke of his parents' hardship, of how his father had scraped together what money he had and bought a small house in Hampshire. "That is where I was born," he added.

Nella recalled the way the major had looked yesterday when she asked whether he had been a boy in Hampshire. She could not help protesting, "But at least they loved each other."

He gave a short bark of laughter. "Not for long, alas. My father tried to find work, but he was a gentleman and unused to labor. My mother took in language and music students, then turned seamstress. She tried everything she could, and yet there was little money. My father became bitter and angry. Later, he was merely indifferent. By the time he died, my parents were like two strangers living under the same roof."

Nella caught her lip between her teeth. She could hardly imagine the sterile misery of such an existence. The Lindens had been poor in the last few years of Sir Tom's life, yet they had been rich. Sir Tom and Lady Elizabeth had loved each other and their children.

To live without love was terrible. Nella did not realize she had spoken her thought aloud until the major spoke dryly. "It's worse to live without money. That is why I agree that your stepmother should marry Moore."

"And you, also, intend to marry a moneyed lady?" Nella knew that this was a highly personal question, but the major did not seem offended.

"That time is far off. But yes, you are right. Marriage should be a contract that benefits both parties. I will never follow my father's example, I can promise you."

The harsh note in his voice made her catch her lower lip between her teeth. "*How* did you survive those bitter years?"

He shrugged. "It does a man good to live by his wits. Poverty teaches him to rely only on himself. One of my mother's relations left me a small inheritence, and with it I was able to make Mother comfortable. For myself, I bought a commission. Fortunately, there was a war, and death being democratic, I rose swiftly through the ranks." He paused, and a smile softened his hard mouth. "I'm glad of one thing. My mother's last years were peaceful, even happy."

Instinctively, she reached out and placed her hand on his arm. "I am glad, too," she said. "Your mother must have been a very brave lady. And—and I think you are brave also."

Her touch carried warmth and understanding. Her voice, her words seemed to burrow deep into Harcourt, touching a portion of his heart that he had almost forgotten. Something seemed to shiver into life within him, and he almost covered her small hand with his own. Then he noted that Nella Linden's glove had been mended in three places.

Harcourt shook his mind free of mist and moonshine and spoke bracingly, "You are talking fustian, ma'am. I've enjoyed the life of a soldier. In fact, I have been thinking that peace can be tedious. Since Napoleon is stirring up trouble again, my regiment may be called into action."

"I understand," she said. "You are a practical man.

If Sir Tom had had as much sense as you have, we would not be up the River Tick."

"Then let me be of some use to you. We can be allies, Miss Linden."

She looked up at him in surprise. "Allies?"

"I'll be honest with you. I brought my friend Deering to rusticate in Hampshire so that he could forget his fatal attraction to Lady Barbara Hinchin. Now that he has found another goddess to adore, it will be safe for him to return to London."

"After he has amused himself with Angel, you mean? But that must not be!"

"Remember that we are allies," he replied. "I don't want Deering to form an unsuitable attachment that will cause everyone grief, so I will keep him away from Lady Linden until we leave for London." He paused and added lightly, "Alas, that also means I will not have the pleasure of your company after today, Miss Linden."

Nella noted that the major was once again speaking in his old, easy fashion. She felt relieved that he had agreed to help her, and yet in some shadowy, inexplicable way, she felt a twinge of loss.

"I will be most obliged to you," she told the major firmly. "Now, let us ride. Excalibur is longing to stretch his legs."

She tapped her heels against Excalibur's sides and sent him flying away from Harcourt and past the earl's curricle. But though the black stallion ran as fast and as free as the wind, Nella could not shake off the dull pain in her heart.

# Chapter Seven

"One does not wish to boast," droned Lord Moore, "but it is true that the grapes that grow on my Sussex estate are far superior to those grown elsewhere. After all, one has devoted years to the study of horticulture. Growing fruit is an art indeed."

Nella hid a yawn behind her embroidery. She had been up since before dawn helping Torfy with the boarded horses, and then there had been a riding lesson. The weather was March-cold and the wind March-brisk, and hard work and the sun-warmed morning room was making her feel sleepy.

Lord Moore's conversation was also soporific. One grew so much grain in Hampshire and enjoyed a plentiful harvest of apples in Sussex. The hunting was fine in one's estates in Scotland, which abutted the vast holdings of no less a personage than the old and eccentric but very rich Viscount Arann. One did not want to boast, but one's Scottish estates did not suffer *much* in comparison to Arann's.

Nella glanced at her stepmother and saw that Angelica's eyes had glazed over. Something had to be done or Lord Moore's discourse on the raising of superior fruit would be interrupted by unladylike snores.

She set down her embroidery. "I collect, my lord," she said brightly, "that the Season will soon be upon us. Do you intend to remove to your London town house?"

Interrupted in mid-sentence, Lord Moore frowned, but Angelica revived somewhat. "London must be beautiful in the spring," she began hopefully.

"Spring is far more satisfactory in Hampshire," his lordship replied. "One is not in the habit of frequenting the city during the Season."

"Indeed?" Nella wondered. "Why so?"

"One does not expect young ladies to be aware of what takes place in large cities. It grieves me to tell you that dissipation and crime are rife in the city."

"But surely," Angelica protested timidly, "there are beautiful parts of London? I collect that Sir Tom very much enjoyed going to the theater. He promised to take me there when we visited Colonel and Mrs. Karmer in London—they are dear friends of ours—but he died before he could keep his promise."

"One is glad that you were not subjected to the experience," Lord Moore declaimed. "The theater is patronized by fribbles who squander their money and their time on vanity. They paint their faces with lead and stain their hands with walnut juice or else drive their curricles recklessly through the streets without a care for others. Believe me, my lady, London is no place for decent people."

Looking dashed, Angelica subsided. Nella said

peaceably, "We are used to living in the country, so we are ignorant of city ways."

"That is to be expected." Lord Moore deliberately adjusted the lapels of his coat of light gray superfine before adding, "For all its glitter, London is not gold. One could say that the city is like a man without principles who *cannot* be called a gentleman, no matter how high his connections."

Seeing Angelica's eyes cloud over, Nella felt a twinge of guilt. Lord Moore's less than subtle allusion to the Earl of Deering was a reminder that the earl had not called at Linden House for an entire week. Though Angelica had had many admiring visitors, Major Harcourt had kept his friend away.

As Lord Moore prosed on, Nella considered that last outing with Harcourt. "We are allies," he had said, and no doubt that was why she missed him. The major was one man with whom she could be totally honest. He never seemed shocked at what she said, and he understood what poverty was. After a steady diet of Lord Moore, it would have been refreshing to talk sense with the major.

The front door banging open startled Nella out of such thoughts, and next moment Rosemary's excited voice floated through the house. "Oh, Stubbs, the most famous thing has happened," she cried. "Is Nella with Angel? I must tell them at once."

Next moment, she had burst into the morning room. "Nella, Angel," she cried, "I have such news—"

She stopped short as the hem of her skirts caught Lord Moore's cane, which was standing by his chair.

It bounced into an occasional table, which teetered over and upended his lordship's glass of lemonade.

"Oh, I *am* sorry," Rosemary exclaimed. "What a guy I am!"

She went down on her knees to retrieve the glass. Unfortunately, Lord Moore also bent down for the same purpose. There was a sharp, cracking sound as their heads collided.

"Confusion take it," Rosemary yelped.

She straightened up and began massaging her head so that her already windswept hair stood all over her head. Lord Moore's eyes grew forbidding, and the bow he swept her was almost arctic. Rosemary looked nervous and stammered, "I b-beg your pardon, sir. I d-did not know you were here. I was sketching out in the woods, you see, and did not see you drive up."

Lord Moore sniffed, and Nella felt a spurt of impatience. His lordship might be necessary to their plans, but really, there was no reason for the man to glump continuously at Rosa.

"No harm is done," she said. "Do come and sit with us, Rosa, and tell us your news."

Rosemary turned to her sister eagerly. "Nella, it is too wonderful. What do you think? Lady Portwick is inviting us to her Great Supper."

Nella and Angelica exchanged startled glances. Lady Portwick's Great Supper was an annual occasion that took place at the end of March. It was an exclusive event, limited to those whom Lady Portwick deemed worthy of special regard, and to be invited was accounted something of a coup among the local gentry.

Lord Moore looked down his thin nose. "One cannot but feel that Lady Portwick gives herself airs that are not wholly appropriate," he commented acidly. "The merits of her Great Supper, I fear, are much exaggerated."

Nella thought that Lord Moore had probably never been invited to the prestigious event. Aloud she said, "You are chasing rainbows, Rosa. We have lived in Hampshire for years, and Lady Portwick has not once thought to invite us. Why should she do so now?"

"I do not know," Rosemary admitted, adding, "but Lionel told me so today while we were sketching together."

Lord Moore's thin brows quivered like startled antennae. "Without a chaperon? How unwise, Miss Rosemary."

The same thought had been hovering in Nella's mind, but now she sprang to her sister's defense. "Rosemary and Lionel have been friends since childhood."

"But they are no longer children. One must observe the correct forms, ma'am, even in the country. Otherwise, we would all be barbarians."

With some effort Nella choked down the retort that rose to her lips. Making some excuse, she left the room and stood in the hallway for a moment to control herself. Then she walked briskly into the kitchen where Mrs. Brunce was making tea.

The Welshwoman looked up from cutting bread

and remarked, "Now, then, Miss Nella, my little one. Why do you have a face like gooseberries with you?"

Nella puffed out her cheeks. "Lord Moore is the outside of enough. He criticizes us and gives us directives. Good God, he is not our father."

"If he marries my lady, he will be your stepfather," Mrs. Brunce pointed out.

The thought was not a new one, but today it was distasteful. "Why was his stiff-rumped lordship criticizing you?" Mrs. Brunce wanted to know.

"I admit that there was some cause for criticism. Rosa let slip that she has been out sketching with Lionel Canton." The Welshwoman said nothing, and Nella's brow puckered. "You *knew* about it?"

Mrs. Brunce looked uncomfortable. "I did not see them myself. It was that whispering fool, Torfy, who told me he'd seen Miss Rosa and Mr. Canton sketching together. The boy has some special spot in the woods, it seems."

Nella groaned. "Rosa's reputation will be in shreds. What is to be done with her?"

"That child has grown up too free. After her dear ladyship died, my lord was too careless, you were too young, and I was too busy to see to her upbringing." Mrs. Brunce sighed. "We cannot change Miss Rosa now, can we?"

There was no use arguing with this logic. But later, when Lord Moore, placated by a hearty tea and much attention, had gone, Nella attempted to reason with Rosemary. "You are eighteen and Lionel is seventeen," she said. "You cannot see him when you are alone, Rosa. The countryside will buzz with gossip."

"Let them buzz," Rosemary replied scornfully. "They talk about me anyway. Besides, it is uttermost fudge that Lionel is a threat to my reputation. He is my friend, *and* he says that we will be invited to his mother's Great Supper." She giggled suddenly. "It is all Deering's doing, naturally. He has a *tendre* for Angel."

Angelica flushed to the roots of her hair. "That is not true," she murmured.

Rosemary picked up a leftover piece of bread and butter and began to munch on it. "Yes, it is. Lionel told me that there was a huge dustup when Deering told his sister that we were to be invited. When Lady Portwick refused to do so, Deering threatened that he would go straight back to London. Lady P is counting on him appearing at her supper, so she gave in. I am persuaded that Deering is pining for Angel."

With her eyes on her stepmother's scarlet face, Nella said, "That is enough. There will be no invitation, depend on it. And in the future you will not meet Lionel unless you are properly chaperoned, Rosa. Is that clear?"

Nella seldom spoke so sternly, and Rosemary did not argue. But a few days later when her elder sister was seated at her desk in Sir Tom's study, Rosemary came bounding in.

"Behold," she announced triumphantly. "Here is the invitation."

Nella looked up wearily from the ledgers that she had been attempting once more to balance. It was an impossible task. Sir Tom's books were a nightmare of debits without credits, and Nella had been wondering how they could manage to buy food for the household. The last thing she cared to think about were invitations to Lady Portwick's supper.

Heedless of her sister's mood, Rosemary rattled on. "Shall I read it? Lord and Lady Portwick, etcetera, request the honor of Lady Linden and the Misses Lindens' presence at a supper on the twenty-fifth of March, etcetera. I *told* you it would come."

"We cannot go," Nella said.

Rosemary looked horrified. "Nella, Portwick Hall is full of the most *wondrous* artwork," she cried. "I *must* see those paintings and statues again. Besides, it is not Lady Portwick who has sent the invitation. You may be sure that this was Deering's idea or else Major Harcourt's."

"Flummery," Nella retorted roundly. "Why would the major think to invite us anywhere?"

Rosemary grinned. "Because he likes your company, peagoose. And I know that you like his company, too. I cannot blame you, for the major is *much* more agreeable than that odious Lord Moore." Rosemary ran up to her sister and hugged her, adding, "Pray do not look so stuffy. Let us go and enjoy ourselves and have a good dinner for a change."

On the point of refusing again, Nella paused. Lord Moore's visit today had left Angelica with another bout of the headache. The man haunted Linden House, came calling nearly every day, but he had so far not declared himself.

He needed a push in the right direction. Since he himself was not invited to the Great Supper, it would no doubt upset Lord Moore if Angelica went to Portwick Hall. Especially would he be upset if he thought that Deering had requested that she be invited.

The more she thought of it, the more this idea made sense. "But," Nella cautioned her sister and Angelica later, "we are going for one purpose only. We must make Lord Moore offer for you."

Angelica, who had brightened when the invitation was first delivered, was now quite calm. "You need not continue," she said. "Collect that it was I who told you how the marriage game is played. But what are we going to wear, dearest?"

Together they went upstairs to review the remnants of their wardrobes, and Angelica shook her head in despair. "There is nothing here that can help us. We will have to wear the same clothes as we did to the ball."

"Rosemary and I can do so but not you. You must look magnificent." Nella drew a deep mental breath before surrendering to the inevitable. "We will have to use some of Mother's clothes."

She called Mrs. Brunce, and together they opened a chest that had remained closed for thirteen years. The Welshwoman's face was grimmer than usual as she flung back the lid.

"I never thought to see the bitter day," she muttered.

It had been hard to sell her mother's things, Nella thought, but this was far worse. She could swear that her mother's scent lingered in the dresses that she drew from the chest.

It took an effort to speak normally. "The mauve satin, I think, will serve. Mother was taller than Angel, so it will have to be cut down. The lace has unfortunately yellowed, but we can sew the roses from this other dress onto the bodice." She blinked back hen-hearted tears and met Mrs. Brunce's eyes squarely. "Think of Purvis taking Excalibur."

Once again, the Linden ladies set to mutilating and assembling dresses. Of them all, only Rosemary was cheerful and prattled endlessly on about the fine art at Portwick Hall. "Though," she went on, "it drives me to distraction that the older paintings are covered with fly specks and should be cleaned, and some of the frames are in a really shocking state! Lady Portwick does not know how to care for precious things. She is a Philistine."

Nella looked up at this and warned, "Please try not to say anything or do anything outrageous, Rosa."

"One will do what one can," Rosemary said in her best imitation of Lord Moore. "Are we going to have to hire a carriage again?"

But this proved unnecessary. On the morning of the dinner, a note arrived presenting Deering's compliments and begging the honor of sending his personal carriage for the ladies' convenience. Accordingly, on the night of the dinner, a handsome carriage bearing the earl's coat of arms came rattling up to Linden House, and a bewigged and liveried footman hopped smartly down to set down the steps so that the ladies could mount.

"What did I tell you?" Rosemary demanded. "This

time we will not be received like country cousins."

Her prediction was accurate. Driven in style through the great gates and up to the door of Portwick Hall, Nella watched the haughty servants turn almost obsequious. "Heigh-ho," continued the delighted Rosemary, "this is *much* more the thing."

Raising her nose to the skies, she followed her stepmother and sister up the stairs and into the drawing room where Lady Portwick's guests were assembled.

Since only the cream of Hampshire society had been invited, Lady Portwick's guest list was extremely selective. Skimming the faces of these happy few, Nella could not see Lord Moore anywhere. Good, she thought. Hopefully his complacent lordship would finally be shaken into some action.

"Miss Linden—ladies."

Major Harcourt was strolling forward, and Nella's heart gave an odd little jump of joy. She offered him her hand, but instead of shaking it, he bent to touch it with his lips. "Ma'am, my homage," he said. "It is good to see you again."

The words and kiss were mere courtesy. Nella knew this. There was no reason for either the pleasure or the confusion that were sweeping through her, and she was grateful when Harcourt turned to greet Angelica and Rosemary, who said frankly, "Major Harcourt, why have we not seen you lately? Have you tired of our company?"

"Never," he replied. "I regret it deeply, Miss Rosa. Deering's at fault—he has been forcing me to hunt and shoot with him."

"Where *is* the earl tonight?" Angelica murmured.

"In captivity." Harcourt's face was grave, but his eyes danced. "Lord Portwick has taken Deering into the Green Room to discuss the merits of a particular bottle of port."

Just then, Lord Portwick ambled into the room with Deering in tow. Nella noted that the earl's bored expression was replaced with eagerness the moment he saw Angelica.

As he pushed ahead of his host and hurried across the room toward them, Nella muttered, "I should have thought that he would have forgotten Angel by now."

Harcourt had thought so, too. They had hunted and gone shooting together. They had attended a turtle supper and a rout at the Viscount Liens's, where Deering had met many eligible and beautiful young ladies.

"It seems as though Deering has been smitten by Lady Linden," he told Nella. As the earl bowed his fair head worshipfully over Angelica's hand, he added, "Don't be alarmed. We're leaving Hampshire very soon."

It was idiotish, Nella told herself, to feel regret, especially since she wanted to keep Deering away from Angelica. "Then you return to London?" she asked.

"Deering does. I plan to rejoin my regiment shortly."

Troubled, she looked up at him. "Then is there definitely to be more fighting?"

"Perhaps, but it is nothing that need trouble you.

Now, tell me about Excalibur. And how goes the sketching, Miss Rosa?"

It was probably because she had been forced to spend so much time with Lord Moore that Nella enjoyed the major's easy conversation. She also liked the way he included Rosemary and did not make her feel like a brass-faced hoyden. When Lionel approached them, Major Harcourt greeted the boy kindly and put him at his ease.

The major was a kind man, Nella thought. Then, out of the corner of her eye, she saw Lady Portwick bearing down upon them and stifled a sigh. Here was one who wished the Lindens no kindness.

Tonight the lady was dressed in an armazine skirt of blue velvet. Sapphires glittered at her throat and in her ears, and her eyes were as hard as the stones as she said sourly, "Lady Linden, how charming to see you again. Miss Linden, your dress is delightful. No wonder you continue to wear it. Miss Rosemary, I see that you have been painting again."

She was staring pointedly at a faint smear of paint on Rosemary's skirt. No amount of scrubbing had removed that spot, and Nella had hoped that it would not show. Determined that Lady Portwick not find fault with *their* manners, she swept a curtsey.

"It is kind of you to invite us, ma'am," she said.

"It was my brother's idea, Miss Linden" was the dismissive reply.

There could be no reply to this. As her ladyship moved away, Deering said gloomily, "M'sister's a griffin, give you m'word. Beg you won't let her tongue spoil your evening, Lady Linden."

"It is of no consequence," Angelica replied.

Angelica's eyes were luminous, her smile radiant. As Deering offered her his arm and walked her away to an alcove, Nella started to follow them.

Harcourt held her back. "Leave them alone," he commanded.

"But—"

"Your stepmother is a grown woman. There are at least thirty people in the room. You need not be on your guard tonight, my dear ally."

Nella glanced at Angelica, who was laughing at something the earl had said, and then at Rosemary, who was deep in conversation with Lionel. "I feel," she sighed, "so responsible."

The troubled look in her eyes made Harcourt want to put a comforting arm around her. This disquieted him. In the days that he had kept Deering from Linden House, he had told himself that he was acting for the earl's good. He now realized that he had been acting out of self-preservation.

Nella stirred him in ways that he could not understand and did not want to analyze. "That is nonsense," he said aloud. "People are only responsible for their own actions."

"Perhaps, but it is not easy to watch those you love do things that might hurt them."

"Then don't look at them." Harcourt slid his arm through Nella's and deliberately executed an about-face. "Is that better?"

She could not help laughing. "No!"

"Forget about your family, I say. Look at how our hostess is glaring at our host. He is consuming another glass of that port I described to you earlier and will be drunk long before dinner."

Perhaps because of this unfortunate tendency in her spouse, Lady Portwick had decided that tonight they should keep country hours and dine before the dancing commenced. Even so, by the time dinner was announced, Lord Portwick could hardly navigate a straight line. He barely managed to seat his fulminating spouse and then drop into his own chair so that the assembled guests could begin their meal.

'Meal' was an inadequate description. No wonder, Nella thought, that this was called a Great Supper. She had never seen so much food before. There were several courses, each with six or seven dishes. There was a sole in a delicate sauce, oysters en escallope, jellied eels, and pickled crab. There were cutlets and chicken and venison; there were veal and hare, mutton and lamb and capons done up in a pastry. Finally, there were sweetmeats, gooseberry tarts in custard sauce, candied fruits and cakes and comfitures and chocolates.

Nella had been hungry when Harcourt took her in to supper, but this mountain of food almost destroyed her appetite. A small portion of this food would feed the entire Linden household for a week. Nella looked to see if Angelica had had the same reaction and saw that her stepmother had eyes only for the earl.

She strained to hear what the earl was saying and was reassured when she heard him talking about horses to a peer seated nearby. " 'Struth, Nyeford," the earl was exclaiming, "that roan of yours don't hold a candle to Lady Linden's black stallion."

He turned doting eyes on Angelica, who protested. "Excalibur is not really mine. He is my elder stepdaughter's."

Instantly the attention shifted to Nella, and Lord Nyeford said, "Rumor has it that he's very fast. Have you plans to race him, Miss Linden?"

Nella was aware that several personages had turned to hear her answer. These were gentlemen and ladies who had placed their bets alongside Sir Tom at Newmarket.

"No," she replied. "I do not intend to race Excalibur."

"B'dad, that's a shame," Deering protested. "Fine animal like that'd take a fat purse at Newmarket. Give you m'word he would. Back him myself any day."

"So would I," exclaimed a marquis seated near the head of the table. "A year ago I watched your jockey training Excalibur for his maiden race. Magnificent animal. Put a wager on him, in fact, but he scratched."

He had been scratched because of Sir Tom's death. Not wanting to discuss that painful subject, Nella said, "Excalibur is not being trained as a racehorse any longer."

"No doubt you need him for your work," Lady Portwick cut in. "I collect that many of you do not know that Miss Citronella Linden gives riding lessons. What a clever young lady you are, to be sure."

Her tone dripped false honey. Nella felt her cheeks grow hot, but she replied as calmly as she could. "I thank you, ma'am, but I fear the praise is undeserved."

"You are too modest." Her eyes sparkling with sugared venom, Lady Portwick continued, "You have a most interesting family, Miss Linden. Miss Rosemary, I am informed, paints."

Rosemary was now the focus of attention. Seated somewhere near the end of the table between a large matron in puce and a gray-haired clergyman, she was attacking a large pasty stuffed with capon.

"You are an artist, are you not, Miss Linden?" Lady Portwick went on. "You paint pictures."

Rosemary attempted unsuccessfully to swallow the large forkful she had just put in her mouth. "I try to do so, ma'am," she mumbled.

"I think you are a clever girl," Lady Portwick said approvingly. "Very gifted indeed."

What was the woman leading up to? Nella looked apprehensively at Harcourt, who was sitting across from her, but the major only shrugged slightly.

Lady Portwick continued. "As you know," she said, "we have a great many works of art here at Portwick Hall. They are the legacy of Portwick's papa, who was a connoisseur of such things. Unfortunately, some of them are in need of cleaning, and the frames require repair. I have tried to remedy the problem, but you know how these tradespeople are." She paused and added silkily, "Perhaps *you* would undertake the work, Miss Rosemary. Naturally, I would pay you a fair wage."

So that was her game. The woman was insulting

Rosemary by equating her to a lowly tradesperson. But before Nella could speak, Rosemary cried, "Ma'am, I should like that above all things. How kind of you to ask me."

Apparently this was not the reaction her ladyship had expected. Harcourt watched sardonically as his hostess began to squirm. She had wanted to humiliate Rosemary but not to engage her services. She had expected chagrin and embarrassment, not enthusiastic agreement.

Oblivious of the fork she was still holding, Rosemary clasped her hands together. "I can start tomorrow. What time shall I come?"

"Hoist with her own petard," Harcourt mouthed at Nella.

The thought made Nella feel quite cheerful, and she was able to do justice to a fruit tart on her plate. But later, when the ladies had left the gentlemen to their port and cigars, she asked Rosemary if she truly wanted to work under Lady Portwick.

"Depend upon it," she warned, "that woman will do all she can to make your life miserable. She will drive you to distraction with her demands. Nothing will satisfy her."

"She can glump at me all day for all I care," Rosemary replied cheerfully. "If only you knew how much I have wanted to be near those paintings! I will be all right, Nella. Lionel will be there to help me."

Rosa could have wished for a better champion, but Nella held her peace. She also bit her tongue when she heard Angelica humming as they went into the drawing room where the dancing was to be held.

Even when Deering came at once to Angelica's side to beg the honor of the first dance, Nella remained silent.

She watched Angelica dance the cotillion with Deering, saw Harcourt standing up to Lady Leigh, and felt unaccountably depressed. All she could hope for was that Lord Moore would be treated to a vivid account of how Lady Linden enjoyed herself at the Grand Supper.

As if to give his lordship more reason for uneasiness, Deering engaged Angelica for the waltz that immediately followed the cotillion. Nella heard a step behind her chair and thought Rosemary had come up behind her. "How graceful Angel looks," she murmured.

"The difference between you and Lady Linden is that she was taught how to dance and you were not," Harcourt's voice replied. When she looked up in surprise, he added, "But better late than never."

"What does that mean?"

"I mean, my dear ally, that I intend to waltz with you. The steps are not difficult for someone who teaches brats to ride."

Nella saw that he was in earnest and shook her head vigorously. "I cannot. There is no use looking at me like that. I would tread on your feet, and besides, Lady Portwick is watching us. Best that you dance with another lady, Major."

"I have no desire to dance with another lady, and even Lady Portwick's dragon eyes cannot see us if we conduct our lesson behind the row of palms in front of the French windows. Last week Colonel

Blighton refuged there for several hours before his wife found him." When she shook her head once more he added, "I never thought you would fight shy."

Nella frowned.

"Can it be that Miss Nella Linden is hen-hearted?" he goaded. "Afraid of Lady Portwick's tongue?"

"Of course not!"

"Ah. Then let me put you to the test."

The major caught Nella's hands and whirled her out of her chair and behind the row of palms. It was done so swiftly that she had no chance to protest. "Now attend," he commanded, "the beat of the waltz is simple. Listen to it and move your feet like this."

She frowned doubtfully. "It does not seem too complicated."

He said, "Let's see what kind of a student you are," and put his arm around her waist.

His arm was strong and sure. His hand in hers conveyed warmth and confidence. Nella felt a wave of sensation that she could neither identify nor explain.

"This is not so easy," she protested.

"Move with me. Keep your neck high, your chin up."

"I am not riding a horse, Major!"

"Both involve balance, control, position, and poise. Feel the music in your bones and let yourself go."

It wasn't the music that Nella felt. It was Harcourt's arm around her waist, his nearness. Though he held her apart from him, there was something in his voice that drew her closer. She felt a wave of light-headedness overcome her as she felt her feet begin to move with the music.

"You are doing it," he said softly. "Relax, Cinderella."

"I am trying, but—*what* did you call me?"

He laughed. "Deering once made a mistake with your name. I find it charmingly apt. You have come to the ball, haven't you?"

All at once Nella felt relaxed and carefree. As the major whirled her up and down the floor behind the shelter of the palms, she felt the odd sensation of being safe in his arms. It was an odd feeling, as unfamiliar as it was heady. Nella was not used to feeling *protected*.

Harcourt had told himself that he would not spend too much time with Nella, but he had been unable to stop himself. He had definitely not meant to ask her to dance, and yet he had been drawn to her as surely as a moth to a flame. That flame was sweeping through him now.

All the careful logic with which he had barricaded his emotions had melted away. Harcourt felt as though the ground had disappeared from beneath his feet. The drawing room and all the people in it seemed to have vanished into smoke, and there remained in the world only this woman with the warm smile and the emerald-green eyes. He swung her about the floor feeling as dazed as a callow youth with his first love.

The music was about to end, but he could not bear to release Nella yet. The dazzlement within him would not permit him to let her go. Obeying an instinct that had nothing to do with common sense, Harcourt waltzed Nella through the French windows and out onto the dark balcony.

The cold March air felt warm to Nella, and the laughter and talk in the drawing room seemed a world apart. All that existed now, here, was the pounding of her heart and the look on Charles Harcourt's face as he bent toward her.

Her eyelashes swooped down over her eyes, veiling them as his mouth came down on hers. His lips were cool and sure and filled her with sensations she had never dreamt of possessing. Nella felt as though she were waltzing into the sun.

"Cinderella," the major murmured against her mouth. "My Cinderella—"

There was a little stir in the darkness near them, the sound of a gasp. "No, my lord, I beg you," Angelica's agitated voice implored.

Harcourt stopped kissing Nella. Nella stiffened in the major's arms. Neither moved nor even breathed as Deering's impassioned voice came floating out of the dark.

"But, Angelica, you don't understand," the earl was saying. "I *love* you."

# Chapter Eight

"I LOVE YOU," repeated the earl fervently. "Knew it the night of the ball. M'heart's yours, beautiful Angel. Worship the ground you walk on, give you m'word."

Nella felt as if she had been drenched with ice-cold water. Rendered numb with shock, she stood rooted to the spot as Angelica protested, "I pray you will not to say such things to me. We—we must return to the others or our absence must be remarked."

"Not till I tell you what's in m'heart," the impassioned Deering vowed. "I will love you till I die."

Damned young fool, Harcourt thought.

Then he realized that he was still clasping Nella to him. He dropped his arms hastily just as an acid voice behind them commented, "So this is where you are, Deering."

Lady Portwick, accompanied by her spouse, stood framed in the French windows. Her arms were folded across her generous bosom, and even in the darkness, Nella could see the look of triumph on her face.

"So," Lady Portwick declaimed, "this is how you comport yourself in my house. The moment my back is turned, you behave yourself shamelessly."

Lord Portwick, who was hovering behind his wife, said, "Quite ri'," and hiccuped.

Nella opened her mouth to speak, but the major's hand squeezed her shoulder. When she looked up at him, she saw him shake his head. Say nothing yet.

"Stubble it, Maria," Deering was retorting wrathfully. "I'm not comporting myself, damn it. Besides, this ain't what it looks like."

"Indeed."

The scorn in Lady Portwick's voice would have melted an iceberg. Angelica covered her face with her hands.

"I *cannot* believe," Lady Portwick continued blightingly, "that a descendant of Saint Hugh the Brave would so forget himself. Deering, you have lessened the honor of your blood by falling into the net of a fortune hunter."

"Maria, if you say another word, I warn you I'll—"

"A fortune hunter, " Lady Portwick continued inexorably, "who is of negligible rank and family. She has set her cap for a wealthy husband and has no qualms about how to get one. Depend upon it, this woman has schemed to have you in her toils."

"Now that," Harcourt remarked, "is the outside of enough."

Lord Portwick goggled, and his spouse stared as Harcourt, with Nella on his arm, strolled forward.

"What are *you* doing here?" her ladyship demanded angrily.

"Miss Linden and I are attending her stepmother. Lady Linden is unwell."

Angelica's cheeks had indeed turned waxy white.

Lord Portwick nodded sagely. "Quite ri'. Don't look the thing at all. Look dashed hagged, if it comes to that."

"Lady Linden," Harcourt continued calmly, "felt faint. She naturally sought out her stepdaughter. Miss Linden requested Deering and myself to assist Lady Linden, and so we escorted her out onto the balcony to get some air."

The major's smooth flow of talk had reactivated Nella's brain. "I am persuaded that it was something she ate," she interposed. "I believe it was the crab."

"Definitely the crab," Harcourt agreed. "It had an off taste. Didn't you think so, Deering?"

"To the devil with the crab," the earl snarled. "Maria, you'll apologize to Lady Linden at once, or b'dad, I won't answer for the consequences."

A quiver flowed through every inch of Lady Portwick's ample frame. "I will do nothing of the kind. I do not believe a word of the Bambury Tales you are telling me, Major Harcourt."

"Are you questioning my word, ma'am?"

The major had not raised his voice, but the chill in it was almost palpable. Releasing Nella's arm, Harcourt strode forward to confront Lord Portwick.

"And you, sir," he challenged, "do you also call me a liar?"

Lord Portwick was not so drunk that he did not recognize danger. In great alarm he exclaimed, "Never said sho. Ashk anyone!"

"Your lady wife has intimated that I was not telling the truth about Lady Linden's illness."

Harcourt's voice was now filled with unmistakable menace. "That is a slur, sir, not only on my good name but on Lady Linden's honor. I demand that you allow me satisfaction."

Lord Portwick's eyes bulged like boiled onions. "Shatis—s-satisfaction?" he squeaked. "For—for what, my dear fellow?"

Keeping his gaze riveted on Lord Portwick's agitated face, Harcourt snapped, "Deering, you will act for me?"

"Certainly, Court," the earl replied promptly. "Greatest pleasure in the world."

This was too much for Lady Portwick. "That is insane," she gargled. "Deering, you have taken leave of your senses. You would side with this man against your sister's husband?"

"*This man* saved m'life," Deering gritted. "Lady Linden is a guest in this house. Maria, this time you've gone too far."

"Swords or pistols, sir?" Harcourt demanded.

Lord Portwick was almost shocked into sobriety. He had recalled that Major Harcourt was a soldier and handy with both sword and pistol. He had no intention of being shot or run through because of his wife's tongue.

"Now look here, Harcourt," he was beginning when Angelica turned to Nella and stretched out trembling hands.

"Nella," she moaned, "please take me home."

Nella caught and clasped her stepmother in her arms. Angelica's skin was clammy cold, and her whole body shook with spasms. "She is ill," Nella cried in dismay. "Pray, Major, assist us to the carriage."

"Mishunderstanding, all a dashed mishunderstanding," burbled Lord Portwick. "Take the lady home, eh? Nothing more to be said."

Nella started to walk Angelica toward the front doors, but Harcourt held her back. "There *is* something to be said. I believe that an apology is due Lady Linden."

His eyes held Lady Portwick's, and under that steady gray gaze, the lady's belligerence cooled. She saw that her spouse had beat a hasty retreat into the drawing room and muttered, "I could have been mistaken, perhaps."

"I did not hear you, my lady."

Glaring at Harcourt, Lady Portwick spoke in a louder tone. "I was mistaken. I am sorry if I offended Lady Linden."

"It might be best to inform your guests that Lady Linden is unwell and was forced to leave," Harcourt suggested.

"What can I do?" Deering cried. Concern had wiped out anger, and he looked almost as pale as Angelica.

"Help the ladies to their carriage. I'll find Miss Rosemary."

Propelling the Portwicks before him, Harcourt left the balcony, and Deering turned a distraught countenance on Angelica. "What shall I do? Command me in anything. I'd rather cut m'heart out than see you suffer, m'lady."

Angelica shook her head mutely and buried her

face in Nella's shoulder. "It is best I take her home at once," Nella said, interrupting further protestations.

Deering wished to sweep Angelica up in his arms and carry her down to her carriage, but Nella firmly dissuaded him. "That will only cause talk, and talk is what we must avoid. If you can get the carriage, sir, I will help Lady Linden down the stairs."

Reluctantly, the earl went away, and Angelica sobbed, "Oh, Nella, I am so ashamed. I have disgraced us all."

"You have done nothing of the kind," Nella replied fiercely. "It was all the fault of that horrid woman." And of that rake, her brother, she thought. "Hush, Angel. We will soon be away from this place."

She was truly worried about Angelica. Her cheeks were bloodless, her eyes glazed. She looked as though she would faint at any moment. She leaned heavily on Nella, who staggered under her taller stepmother's weight. Nella was grateful when Harcourt overtook them on the stairs.

Followed by Rosemary, he came swiftly up to them and took Angelica's free arm. "Lean on me, Lady Linden," he said bracingly, "and we will be at the carriage in a moment. Miss Rosa, where is your stepmother's wrap? It won't do to catch cold."

Nella said nothing until they had reached the carriage. Then, leaving Deering to assist Angelica, she turned to the major. "Can Lady Portwick be trusted not to speak of this?" she asked in a low tone.

"Yes." Harcourt's fine lip curled derisively. "Neither she nor her lion-hearted husband will breathe a word. Your stepmother's reputation is safe, Miss Linden."

*Miss Linden.* So she was no longer Cinderella. As the thought registered, Nella could hear Deering stammering, "Beg you to forgive m'behavior—carried away—madness of the moment—"

Nella glanced at the major and saw that his eyes were cool and impersonal. He was no longer the man who had taken her in his arms and kissed her, nor was she the flutter-headed gudgeon who had allowed him to do so. The inexplicable insanity that had possessed them was gone.

"I had better get Deering back to the party," Harcourt was saying. "Good-bye, Miss Linden."

Nella climbed into the carriage, and the major gave the order to the coachman. The moment they were on their way, Angelica burst into heartbroken tears. "Oh," she mourned, "I have been such a fool."

Nella could have cheerfully strangled Lady Portwick. She would also have liked to box the earl's aristocratic ears. She put her arms around her stepmother and rocked her as if she were a child. "Hush, Angel, do not cry so. The major promised me that the Portwicks will hold their tongues."

"Why should they?" Rosemary wanted to know. "What has happened? And what is the matter with Angel? I was in the gallery trying to decide which paintings I would try and rescue first when the major came and *dragged* me away."

"I do not care tuppence for the scandal," Angelica

wept, ignoring Rosemary. "Oh, Nella, I love him."

Nella felt her heart sink to the floor of the jolting carriage.

"I did not want to fall in love with him. I knew we could never suit. But—but he is so kind and gentle to me, and he has such beautiful blue eyes—"

"I have noted those eyes," Rosemary broke in. "As a matter of fact, I had wanted to paint the earl's portrait. He would make a far better Saint Hugh than that pigeon fancier who is displayed in the gallery. But if he has made you weep, Angel, I will never, *never* paint him."

Nella frowned her sister quiet. "Angel," she said bracingly, "you are overwrought. You need a good cup of tea with some of Sir Tom's brandy in it."

With an effort, Angelica pulled herself together. "It is my own fault. I knew that Deering would never offer for me, but I allowed him to lead me out onto that balcony. I—I *wanted* him to kiss me."

For a second Nella recalled the feeling of being held in arms that were strong and yet gentle, that could excite as well as protect. For an instant, she allowed herself to remember the feel of Major Harcourt's lips on hers.

Then she shook her mind free of idiocy. She and the major were both hardheaded realists. What had happened tonight was simply an aberration, one that she would never dwell upon again. There were realities to face.

Realities like the fickle Earl of Deering and prosy Lord Moore, and Purvis. At the thought of Purvis, Nella's eyes hardened.

"Once we get home," she told her stepmother, "Mrs. Brunce will warm your bed with a hot brick, and I will sit by you until you fall asleep. Angel, do not cry. It will all turn out right in the end."

The next morning, early, before her stepmother and sister had risen, Nella stole out of the house, saddled Excalibur, and took him for a gallop through the meadow. After the disastrous events of the previous night, she felt she needed to breathe fresh air and feel Excalibur's strength and eagerness.

"Run, my beauty," she urged him. "Fly!"

Last night in Major Harcourt's arms she, too, had felt as though she had found wings. But now that brief flight was over. Just as Deering would never offer for Angelica, so Harcourt and Nella could never suit. They might be allies, even friends, but marriage had never been an issue.

At least Harcourt had been honest. He had never talked of love like that loose fish, his friend. Nella felt a renewed rush of anger as she thought of Angel crying herself to sleep. She urged Excalibur faster as though she could outrun her troubles, but when they reached the loop in the road, her heart was still heavy.

At the loop, she hesitated. Her riding students would be arriving in two hours' time, and before that she needed to have a long talk with Angelica. Reluctantly, Nella turned Excalibur toward home, but as she did so she heard the sound of wheels behind her on the road. She turned her head and saw that a landau was fast approaching her.

Seated in the landau was Purvis and another man. "An early riser, ain't you, Miss Linden?" Purvis hailed her. "Don't run off, now. We need to talk to you."

"We have nothing to discuss." Nella gritted through her teeth.

By now Purvis was near enough for her to see his sneer. He touched his cheek where her whip had caught him and snapped, "There's a score to be settled, my fine lady."

Nella's fist closed tightly about her riding crop, and as if sensing her mood, Excalibur pawed the ground and tossed his proud head. At this Purvis's companion leaned forward to ask, "Would that be the horse in question, Mr. Purvis?"

Nella took this man's measure. Purvis's companion was a stout man with stubby hands and a coat that would hardly close over his rotund belly. He had the nasal voice of a man with a head cold. Nella loathed him instinctively.

"Whoever you are," she said clearly, "understand that there is no question about the ownership of this horse. He belongs to me."

"So *you* say," Purvis snapped. "Mr. Carminkle here's my solicitor."

The stout man nodded. "I have in my possession some papers which state clearly that Mr. Purvis has a right to his horse. We were on our way to Linden House to meet with you and your stepmother."

A hard knot of anger had wedged itself in Nella's throat. "If you set foot on our land," she warned, "I will have Torfy throw you off."

"We'll see about that," Purvis snarled.

He started to drive his landau forward, but Nella blocked his way. "You will need more proof of ownership than notes on which you forged Sir Tom's signature."

"Grasping at straws, ain't you? You know nothing's been forged." Purvis showed his teeth as he added, "Like it or not, I mean to take the horse today. He'll enter a special handicap they're holding at Newmarket next month."

Nella cried, "If you lay one finger on Excalibur, I will take Sir Tom's pistol and shoot you."

Purvis laughed, but his eyes were cold with anger. "Hellcat, ain't she, Carminkle?"

The fat solicitor's oily chuckle sent Nella over the edge of common sense. She shouted, "You will laugh out of the other side of your mouth when you hear from a gentleman you cannot intimidate. You may be brave in the company of females, but Major Harcourt will know what to do with a counter-coxcomb like you."

She hadn't meant to use Harcourt's name. She had merely remembered how Lord Portwick had cowered before the major's anger. And the magic held. Nella, holding her breath, saw Purvis hesitate.

All his life Purvis had made it his business to listen to gossip around London. He had naturally heard of the Earl of Deering and of the man who had saved the earl's life. Purvis knew that Major Harcourt had been lionized by some of the most influential members of the ton. He knew that the major had a reputation as a man with iron nerves, a man who would not cut his stick at anything.

Like all bullies, Purvis was a coward. He scowled as Nella warned, "Do not dare to show your face near Linden House if you value your skin."

Rapping out a vicious oath, Purvis sawed his horses' heads around. Then, turning in his seat, he shook his fist at Nella. "You ain't seen the end of this. I'm going to have that horse, Miss Hellcat, one way or another."

Nella's stomach felt queasy as she watched Purvis and his solicitor ride away. She knew that she had only postponed the inevitable. After his set-to with the Portwicks, Harcourt was sure to leave Hampshire. When he learned of her supposed protector's departure, Purvis would be back.

Slowly she rode back to Linden House, where Torfy was mucking out the stalls of the boarded horses. There was no sign of Rumtum or the old barouche.

"Eh, Miss Rosa, tha looks like tha's seen a flay-boggart," Torfy exclaimed in his die-away voice. "Art all reet?"

She nodded and asked, "Where is Rumtum?"

"Miss Rosa took him up to Portwick Hall. She left a half hour since. But, ma'am, what ails tha? Canst hardly walk."

Reaction made Nella ache in every limb. It took an effort to square her shoulders and walk toward the house where Angelica was breakfasting alone in the morning room. An uneaten egg in its shell stood before her, and a cup of watery tea. Mrs. Brunce, standing behind Angelica's chair, was scolding her.

"Eat nothing and you will waste away, indeed to God. *Ach y fy*, my lady, you will make yourself sick."

Forlorn as a white statue, Angelica simply sat there. "Bruncie," Nella interposed, "will you be a dear and make me a cup of tea? I am not hungry, either."

Muttering worriedly under her breath, Mrs. Brunce returned to the kitchen. "Angel, how are you?" Nella asked.

Angelica sighed deeply and looked out of the window in the direction of Portwick Hall. "How would *you* feel?"

*Desperate*, Nella thought. Aloud she said, "Angel, forget about last night. We have other troubles. I met Purvis on the road to town, and he wants to enter Excalibur in a special handicap at Newmarket. Unless we can borrow some money and pay off Sir Tom's note, Excalibur will be his."

Just then, Stubbs entered with an envelope that he presented to Angelica. She turned paler than before and murmured, "It is from Lord Moore. Why should he write me a letter?"

"Open it and you'll see, my lady." Mrs. Brunce had come in with the tea. "The boy who brought that note has another bit of news," she added conversationally. "He says he passed the Earl of Deering's curricle, now just. His lordship and his valet and all his baggage was driving along the road to London. Major Harcourt was with him."

Angelica's hand tightened convulsively about the knife with which she was slitting Lord Moore's envelope, but Nella was not surprised at Mrs. Brunce's revelation. She owned herself relieved that Deering had gone, but in spite of the relief there was a small, gnawing ache beneath her breastbone.

Ignoring the ache, she asked, "What does Lord Moore say?"

"He seeks permission to call on me today." Angelica attempted to smile. "I collect that you were right and that his lordship means to declare for me. I must look my best when he arrives."

She got to her feet, lurched blindly against the breakfast table, and groped her way to the door. Nella jumped up and caught her stepmother's hands in hers.

"Angel, if there was any other way—"

"But there is not. I know." Angelica's smile made Nella want to cry. "It does not matter, dearest. *He* has gone, as we all knew he would. I—I will stop being a fool."

Nella wanted to put her arms around her stepmother and hug her close. She wanted with all her heart to shout out that Angelica need not accept Lord Moore. But the words died on her lips as she remembered Purvis and the way he had eyed Excalibur. Purvis would race Excalibur and race and race him till the black stallion's great heart burst from exhaustion.

Nella's own heart felt very heavy as she went about her tasks. Then, about to go out to instruct her riding students, she opened the door and came face-to-face with Lord Moore.

She had not heard him drive up and was surprised to see him so early. She noted that his lordship was today dressed in a well-fitting, if somewhat old-fashioned, blue jacket. His ruffled shirt was so white that it seemed to reflect light. His breeches were of fine buckskin and his boots had been polished until they shone like mirrors. If not in the kick of fashion, Lord Moore had definitely dressed for an occasion.

"Ah," he said. "Good morning, Miss Linden. Are you riding?"

"No, I am about to start my lessons." Nella noted the disapproval in his lordship's slight frown and felt a familiar stab of irritation. Naturally, Lord Moore would disapprove of a lady stooping to work for a living.

"You wished to see my stepmother," she said as cordially as she could. "She is in the morning room."

He bowed then checked himself to ask primly, "Might one be so bold as to request to see her ladyship alone? I have words that are for Lady Linden's ears alone."

So, Nella thought, he *had* come to declare himself. But instead of the rush of hope and gratitude she had expected, she felt a heaviness in her heart. It's the only way, she told herself as she instructed Stubbs to lead his lordship to Angelica. Lord Moore might be a bore, but he was not a bad man. He would be kind to Angel.

Her young students were waiting for her, and the riding lessons began. Usually, Nella could lose herself in her teaching, but today her thoughts were far afield. If only, she thought, Angelica had never met Deering. Or, failing that, if only Lord Moore had one ounce of the earl's charm and address—

Suddenly, the front door of the house banged open and Lord Moore came storming out. His lordship had not even bothered to put on his hat or his gloves, and he cursed his groom loudly.

What could have possibly happened? Leaving Torfy to continue the riding lessons, Nella dismounted and hurried toward the house. On the way, Lord Moore's perch phaeton almost bowled her over. He made no apology. In fact, she doubted if he had even seen her.

"What in the world?" she exclaimed.

Mrs. Brunce now poked her head through the open door. "Miss Nella," she shouted, "come quick! Her ladyship looks ready to faint."

Nella ran past the Welshwoman and into the morning room. Angelica was sitting on the sofa with her hands clasped in her lap. She had gone so pale that even her lips were white.

Nella dropped onto her knees beside her stepmother and gripped her icy hands. "What did he do to you?" she demanded fiercely. "Tell me."

"I have just refused Lord Moore," Angelica said.

Nella let go of Angelica's hands and sat down hard on the ground. "You *refused* him?"

"Nella, he said that though our stations in life were unequal, he still wished to marry me." Hot color flooded into Angelica's face, and her usually gentle eyes snapped with indignation. "He said that *proper restraint* would soon change Rosa's wild and wayward ways. And he dared to add that once he was master of this household, you would not be permitted to give riding lessons like a cit."

"Did he, just?" Mrs. Brunce snarled. "Master of the house, indeed. Torfy and me will go after him in the cart, now just, and bring him back to apologize to you."

"Wait," Nella commanded sternly. "Angel has not finished. What else did he say?"

"H-he said that he had heard about my unwise behavior with D-Deering, but that he was not one to listen to g-gossip." The angry color faded from Angelica's face, and tears trembled in her eyes. "Oh, Nella, he said it in such a nasty way that I was sure he would throw my—my indiscretion at my head forever."

"A pox on him," Nella cried.

For once Mrs. Brunce did not protest Nella's using one of Sir Tom's oaths.

"How dare he think he can come and order us about and—and how *dare* he criticize you?" Nella's green eyes blazed like emeralds. "May the devil fly off with him."

Taking a determined breath, Angelica said, "You mean that I should encourage Mr. Hampton."

"I mean nothing of the sort. You do not need to marry anyone you do not love, Angel, nor will you. There is another way."

Nella got to her feet and faced her family. "We will enter Excalibur in the special handicap at Newmarket," she announced. "We will put everything we own on his back. And we will *win*!"

# Chapter Nine

Angelica stared at her stepdaughter. "But, Miss Nella, my little one," Mrs. Brunce stammered, "you swore never to set foot in Newmarket again."

"That was then and this is now," Nella declared adding, "let me *think*."

She sat down on the faded sofa beside Angelica and attempted to pull her tumbled thoughts into some logical sequence. Just before Sir Tom died, Excalibur had been ready to race his maiden race at Newmarket. He had been withdrawn.

"Excalibur is eligible for the special handicap," Nella said. "And depend upon it, if Purvis wants to enter him for the special handicap, there is a heavy purse. Where is Stubbs?"

The butler appeared as if by magic. He had apparently withdrawn out of sight but not out of earshot, and all his years of training could not erase the martial light in his faded old eyes.

"What may I do, Miss Nella?" he pleaded.

"Will you please tell Torfy that I want him? I must contact Ableman at once."

Ableman was the jockey who had ridden so many

of Sir Tom's horses to victory during the glory days. He had been present on the night that Excalibur was foaled. Nella had no doubt that Ableman would set aside whatever he was doing so that he could ride Excalibur in his maiden race.

As Stubbs hastened away, Mrs. Brunce shook her head.

"Foolishness, indeed to God. Sir Tom brought ruin on this house by betting at that Newmarket. I never thought to see the day when you would follow in his footsteps, Miss Nella."

Angelica covered her face with her hands and commenced rocking back and forth. "It is my fault for rejecting Lord Moore," she keened.

"Fustian." Nella shot to her feet and nervously began to pace the room. "I tell you, we can carry it off. We can wipe out a great many of Sir Tom's debts in one race. There is the purse. Also, we can place private wagers on Excalibur."

Mrs. Brunce threw up her hands. "*Ach y fy*, it's madness."

"Nay, it's not."

Torfy was standing next to Stubbs at the door of the morning room. "Not madness," he continued. "That gradely horse can run like the wind. Eh, I'll stake my life on his winning."

"Shut up, man," Mrs. Brunce snapped, but Torfy was not to be intimidated.

"Tha may think me a great gowk, Ceridwen Brunce, but horses is summat that I know. I've worked wi' horses, man and boy, for nigh on forty year, and never have I seen a better animal. Nay, he's more human than many men I know. He'll take his maiden race, sithee, or my name's not Peter Torfy."

The groom's voice had gained volume. Now, aware that the others were staring at him, he blushed hotly and ducked his head. In his old, whispery manner he added, "Any road, now is not the time for fratching. We have to support Miss Nella."

Since Torfy's show of spirit seemed to have momentarily silenced Mrs. Brunce, Nella said, "Naturally I do not propose to go to Newmarket alone. I will write to our friend Colonel Karmer in London. He and his wife are among the few people who did not shy away from us when Sir Tom died. Colonel Karmer knows Excalibur and is familiar with the procedures one must follow at Newmarket. He will help me to make the necessary arrangements."

Angelica looked frightened. Mrs. Brunce opened her mouth to speak, then closed it with a snap. Stubbs so far forgot himself as to wish Miss Nella well in her grand venture. "It is almost like the old days," he quavered. "If I may be so bold, ma'am, we must all remember that stout hearts *cannot* fail."

Before the day was out, Nella had written to Colonel Karmer and had sent off a message to her jockey, Ableman. Three days later a small, wiry figure in faded buckskins swaggered up to the servants' door at Linden House. To Mrs. Brunce, who opened the door, he declaimed, "Ah, Ceridwen, me beauty. You're looking lovelier than Fa-rooo's daughters."

Mrs. Brunce was not impressed. "Ah, dammo," she snapped, "what bad wind sent you, indeed?"

Ableman grinned. "Will you tell Miss Nella that I 'ave harrived and will hawait 'er at the stables, me lovely?"

He tipped his cap, winked expressively, and swaggered off to the stables where Nella found him some minutes later. He was in Excalibur's stall, smoothing the black horse's flanks and crooning love words to him.

"What do you think?" Nella asked anxiously.

"I thinks that 'e's as fine as that there 'orse what belonged to that there Halexander the Great" was the answer.

Ableman's sharp, leathery face was pinched with excitement, and his black eyes were as bright as a bird's. Strong hands that had guided the reins of so many horses to victory gentled Excalibur's ebony flanks. When Nella explained the circumstances, he nodded.

"Torfy 'as told me. That Purvis is a wulture what ought to be 'orsewhipped out o' England. We'll see what we can do, Miss Nella. You leave it to me."

Ableman moved into his old quarters above the stable and immediately resumed the training that had been curtailed by Sir Tom's death. Watching from the sidelines with her late father's stopwatch clamped tightly in her hand, Nella was torn between hope and despair.

While she watched Excalibur thunder about the track, her confidence rose almost to fever pitch. At night when she was alone and sleepless, she understood what a terrible gamble she was undertaking. The Lindens had little left, but she was prepared to stake that little and more besides on the hope that the black stallion would make good.

It would cost money to stable Excalibur at Newmarket. It would cost much more to place private wagers on the horse. Nella agonized about this, for she knew that such wagers were necessary. The purse alone would not bring enough to pay off Sir Tom's debts. Was she leading everyone, including Torfy and Ableman, into ruin? She wished that she had someone to advise her. Angelica was too frightened, Mrs. Brunce was too disapproving for impartial counsel, and Rosemary could think of nothing but her work at Portwick Hall to care about. If only Major Harcourt were here, Nella thought.

More than once Nella found herself wishing that the major would come riding up to the door so that she could talk to him. She needed Harcourt's clear, ofttimes cynical logic. He was the one man with whom she could be totally honest, and the one man who would be able to analyze her situation and suggest options. But Major Harcourt was not in Hampshire and perhaps by now he was on his way back to the war, newly kindled by Napoleon.

That thought depressed Nella as much as did several new and threatening missives from Sir Tom's creditors. But a letter from Colonel Karmer at least assured her of some support.

As Nella explained to her family, the colonel and Mrs. Karmer would be proud to assist the widow and daughters of his old friend. The colonel would be glad to escort the ladies to the races, and meanwhile, he would make necessary arrangements for Excalibur and his grooms at Newmarket.

"Torfy and Ableman are to leave for Newmarket several days before the special handicap," she said. "Meanwhile, Mrs. Karmer suggests that we come and stay in London as her guests. She remembers that you wished to go to the theater, Angel, and writes to say that Mrs. Siddons is soon to play Portia at the Theater Royal."

"How kind of Mrs. Karmer to remember that." Looking more animated than she had in days, Angelica added, "I would like to go to London above all things. Do you not think so, Rosa?"

But Rosemary point-blank refused to leave Hampshire. "I cannot go. I am removing fly specks from a fine landscape. It is painstaking work, and even with Lionel helping me it will take me *weeks* to complete."

"You have never been to London," Nella protested.

Rosemary struck a dramatic pose. "Nothing is as important as art," she declaimed. "I will stay here with Bruncie."

For Mrs. Brunce also refused to go to London. "I'll not be a part of any of this," she told Nella firmly. "A girl from the village can act abigail to you and Lady Linden. Someone must stay here and look out for Miss Rosa."

Something in the housekeeper's tone made Nella look sharply at her. "Do not peel eggs with me, please. What has Rosa done to disturb you?"

Mrs. Brunce pursed her lips. "Then I'll be frank, is it? Will it be the art or Master Canton that Miss Rosa finds so exciting?"

Nella was shocked. "But they are children," she protested.

"She's eighteen and the boy a year younger," Mrs. Brunce pointed out. Then, as Nella frowned uncertainly she added, "I'll keep an eye on her, so don't worry. It's you who may find yourself in trouble."

In the week that followed, the Linden ladies made what repairs they could to their wardrobe and Torfy and Ableman began preparations for their departure to Newmarket. Before she and Angelica left for London, Nella shared her greatest concern with Torfy and the jockey.

"Keep clear of Purvis when you get to Newmarket," she warned, to which Ableman replied that he hadn't been born yesterday nor was such a Jack Adams as could be bamboozled by niminy-piminy fribble like Purvis.

Since they had no carriage, the ladies and their newly hired abigail elected to travel by mail coach. It was a long and not overly comfortable ride, but Nella was too preoccupied to mind and Angelica, by turns pale and rosy pink, seemed lost in a world of her own. Even so, they were grateful to reach their destination, where they were met by a round little man with white hair and a ferocious white mustache.

"Bless me, but it's good to see you," he said, shaking hands. "I have not had the pleasure of seeing you for nearly a year—ever since poor old Sir Tom's funeral. Eh? My wife is awaiting you anxiously."

He adjusted the military-cut riding cloak he wore, straightened his beaver, and marched the ladies to a waiting barouche that conveyed them to his fashionable town house in Berkeley Square.

They had hardly entered the ground floor hallway when Mrs. Karmer came flying down the stairs to hug her guests. "*Dear* Angelica, *dearest* Nella," she exclaimed, "how glad I am that you could come to us. It is such a treat to see pretty young faces in the house again, don't you think so, Colonel?"

Nella felt her heart expand at this unfeigned welcome. "Thank you," she said. "We are fortunate to have you as friends."

The emotion in Nella's voice caused the colonel to tug at his mustache. He then hastily smoothed it. He was proud of this mustache, which was all that remained of his distinguished days in the cavalry. Then he had been a slight, slender, whipcord-tough young officer, but now he was as round as his lady. In fact, standing close together, they had the look of contented pouter pigeons.

"Nonsense," the colonel declared. "Bless me, dear young ladies, we're the ones to be glad. My wife has someone to go to the theater with. Extraordinary that anyone'd like to go there—pit's stuffed with cits and the gallery's chock-full of snobs and bag-puddings and smatterers."

"Now, Colonel," Mrs. Karmer reproved complacently, "I *beg* that you will not reveal what a Philistine you are." She slipped an arm through each of her guests' as she added, "We are going to *enjoy* ourselves so much. But now, you must rest for the supper I have planned tonight in your honor."

"Invited Tavore and Chuffey Banks and Lord and Lady Francis," the colonel put in. "Their names may be familiar to you, Miss Nella."

Indeed they were, for Nella had met all these people at Newmarket. They were extremely wealthy and gambled heavily. In fact it was common knowledge that Lady Francis had once tossed a diamond tiara on the table while playing faro and that her lord had lost and won several fortunes both at piquet and at Newmarket.

"Thought it wouldn't do Excalibur any harm to have some exposure with the right people," the colonel went on. "If he's well thought of, he'll not want for backers in his next race. Eh? And his stud fees will triple."

All of which made perfect sense. "I do not know what we would do without you," Nella cried.

Colonel Karmer pinkened and preened a little. "Don't mention it, my dear young lady. Eh? After tonight, there'll be talk about Excalibur all over London."

So intent was she on what the colonel was saying that Nella had not noticed the odd expression that filled her stepmother's eyes. "Tell me," Angelica was now saying, "will there be anyone I know at your supper, ma'am? We met the Earl of Deering in Hampshire. Is he invited?"

Nella glanced sharply at her stepmother, and the colonel and his lady exchanged startled looks. "No, we did *not* invite the earl," Colonel Karmer harrumphed. "Young jacknapes, no better than he should be."

"Do not excite yourself, Colonel, it is bad for your internals, as well you know." Mrs. Karmer took the ladies' arms and led them out of the colonel's hearing. "What he *means* is that Deering's latest escapade with Lady Hinchin has tongues wagging all over London. Hot-blooded, the Deerings, you know, and *most* unreliable when it comes to females. Deering's father was an old rumstick who carried on with an opera singer *half* his age. Nigh on broke his wife's poor heart."

Angelica had gone white to the lips. Nella tried to change the subject, but their hostess was enjoying her gossip.

"Lord Hinchin is reputed to be the *best* shot in London. If it hadn't been for Deering's friend, Major Harcourt, *he* might have been shot for carrying on with that redheaded baggage. As it was, Hinchin shot *poor* Mr. Beasie and had to fly to the continent."

Her heart, Nella told herself, had not jumped at the sound of the major's name. There was no reason for it to do so. "Who is Mr. Beasie?" she asked.

"One of Lady Hinchin's victims. Hinchin shot him through the heart," Mrs. Karmer explained. "As I said, it was *only* due to this Major Harcourt that Deering escaped with a whole skin. I have met the major at the Duchess of Ruddyville's ball and did not care for him."

In spite of herself, Nella murmured, "Indeed, ma'am?"

"He is *much* too clever for me," Mrs. Karmer sighed. "I prefer straightforward gentlemen. Major

Harcourt says one thing while meaning another, which is *most* disconcerting."

Disconcerting indeed. Nella thought of the major as he had been on the night of Lady Portwick's Great Supper. "My Cinderella," he had called her.

Suddenly her cheerful hostess, her stepmother, the colonel, and the comfortable town house seemed to fade away and only the image of Harcourt remained. He was more vivid, more real than anyone there. I miss him, Nella thought.

But her lapse was only momentary, and by the time she and Angelica were shown to their rooms, Nella had expunged the major from her mind. Instead, she thought of how upset Angelica had been when she heard the truth about Deering. In a way, she was glad of it. Sometimes, blunt surgery was the best cure.

She watched her stepmother closely that evening, and was reassured when Angelica appeared to be in good spirits among the Karmers' guests. Her beauty was much admired and many single gentlemen flocked about her.

Others gathered about Nella to discuss Excalibur. "Seems as though Sir Tom's daughter's taking up where he left off," Lord Francis said. His narrow blue eyes glittered with gambling fever as he added, "You were always as good a judge of horseflesh as your father, Miss Linden. I remember that black stallion of yours, too. Noble creature."

"Excalibur is a nonpareil," she agreed. "Ableman, our jockey, tells me that he has never seen a finer animal, and he has ridden many excellent horses.

Excalibur will take his maiden race, Lord Francis."

She repeated this many times that evening, and when the guests had gone, Colonel Karmer said that she had done well. "Francis will go posting off to Newmarket, and he'll tell everybody about Excalibur," he said. "He'll soon be the darling of the track, or I don't know human nature."

Nella went to bed exhilarated and woke up late next morning with a faint headache. Her hostess suggested that a turn or two in Richmond Park would dispel such megrims. "For I am going to rest *all* day in preparation for the theater this evening," she said. "I wish to listen to Mrs. Siddons with a *clear* head. Nella, you and dear Angelica take out the phaeton. The colonel just bought matched bays which are a *pleasure* to drive."

It was not difficult to persuade Nella, who felt great pleasure at being able to drive Mrs. Karmer's smart, chocolate-colored phaeton and its spritely horses. The day was warm and a capricious sun was peering through the clouds. London, so muddy and cold and befogged a month ago, had begun to come into its April glory. White clouds, as soft as swans' down, were wafted by gentle breezes that tugged at daffodils and still-furled tulips.

It was so warm that Angelica let fall the pelisse she had donned over her plain round gown of amethyst cambric. It was not new, but its color matched her eyes, and many gentlemen slowed their horses or carriages to stare at the unknown fair. One young bandbox dandy, dressed in an impossibly wide-shouldered coat of canary yellow, a striped green waistcoat, green trousers, and a neckcloth arranged in startling folds, stared so hard at Angelica that he nearly stepped into the way of an approaching curricle.

"Hi, you, watch where you are going," a familiar voice exclaimed. "B'dad, I nearly ran you over, you young idiot."

Angelica started as though she had been struck by lightning. Her hands in their worn doeskin gloves clasped tightly together as though in prayer as she gasped, "It is Deering!"

As she spoke, the earl's curricle passed them by. He was dressed in a fawn-colored coat and buckskins, and there was a pink rose in his lapel. His handsome young face was flushed as he turned to smile at his beautiful, red-haired companion.

One glance at this lady told Nella why Lady Hinchin had caused so much havoc in male hearts. She carried herself with infinite confidence and was dressed in the first stare of fashion in an India muslin with puckered sleeves. A saucy little chip hat tied with emerald sarcenet ribbons adorned her curls, and a pelisse of the same green hue covered her white shoulders. A strand of rubies, as red as Lady Hinchin's hair, glittered and winked about her proud neck.

Nella's fist tightened on her reins, and the horses jerked their heads in protest. Her low command to them made Deering turn his head. He stared as though at a ghost and exclaimed, "Lady Linden!"

Angelica's slender body jerked spasmodically. As

almost as if she were a marionette, she slowly raised her head and met the earl's ardent gaze.

"M'lady!" Deering was stammering. "I—I hadn't thought you to be in London."

Just then Lady Hinchin leaned forward. Nella noted that a malicious expression sparkled in her black eyes even before she drawled, "Lud, Deering, who are these people?"

The earl did not answer but spoke urgently to Angelica. "If I'd known you were in London, I'd have paid m'respects. What's your direction, Lady Linden?"

Before Angelica could answer, Lady Barbara placed a proprietary hand on the earl's arm. "Deering," she pouted, "this becomes tedious. If you wish to cose with your friends without introducing me, we will fall out."

With obvious reluctance, Deering withdrew his eyes from Angelica and made the introductions. "We met in Hampshire," he added.

Lady Barbara smiled. "That explains it. And to think that Harcourt dragged you there so that he could be cured of love. A ramshackle idea, since the country is so dull and unfashionable and full of homely Joans."

Her black eyes flicked disdainfully over Angelica's dress, over her hair, over her tightly folded hands. It was almost as though she could see the mends in the fingers of her gloves.

Without waiting to hear more, Nella whipped up the horses. As they sprang forward, she could hear

Lady Hinchin drawl, "She is pretty enough, but hardly the beauty you described. Lud, Deering, I am disappointed in your taste."

There was a muted sob beside her, and Nella spoke through gritted teeth. "Angel, if you shed one tear in front of that redheaded jade, I will—I will box your ears."

Angelica gave a tremendous sniff. "How *could* he, Nella? He said he loved me. He swore never to forget me. Now he laughs at me with that woman."

Nella had no comfort to offer. Silently, she turned her horses toward Berkeley Square.

It was a dispirited ride home, and by the time they reached the Karmer's door, Angel looked as sick as she had done on the night of the ball. She took to her bed, and when evening came around, she was feeling much too ill to go to the theater. Mrs. Karmer protested that in that case none of them would go, but Nella would not have this.

"That is fustian, dear ma'am," she said firmly. "You know that you have looked forward to seeing Mrs. Siddons perform. I, too, do not feel quite the thing, so I will stay home with Angel, and you can tell us all about it in the morning."

Mrs. Karmer was reluctant but she *had* looked forward to seeing the famous Siddons as Portia, and she allowed herself to be persuaded. Her carriage rattled away, the colonel went to his club, and the house on Berkeley Square quietened.

Angelica felt too sick to get up, so Nella sat by her bed and read to her from the *Mirror of Fashion*. After a while, Angelica put a hand on her stepdaughter's arm.

"I am sorry, dearest," she said humbly. "I have made you miss *The Merchant of Venice.*"

"I do not care tuppence for the theater," Nella said truthfully. "I am worried about you."

"You need not be," Angelica replied. "I have been a great fool, Nella. I confess that I came to London hoping that *he* would see me and realize that he loved me. This morning has cured me of such idiotish illusions."

Nella stayed with Angelica until at last she fell into a restless sleep. Then, getting to her feet, she stretched her back and went downstairs into the silent house. It was late, and there was no footman at the door.

Nella stared at that massive door. She knew that the best remedy for blue devils was fresh air and exercise. Riding at this time of night was out of the question, but she could still walk and stretch her legs.

Nella reached for her cloak, but when she had opened the door, she hesitated. This was London, not friendly Hampshire. Also, it was very dark, and the fog that swirled about the street gave even familiar objects a ghostly appearance. Nella almost retreated into the house, but then gave herself a mental shake. She was not so hen-hearted that darkness and mist should frighten her.

Taking an umbrella from the stand in the hallway, she walked briskly down the front steps. The fog closed around her and turned her footfalls into unpleasant, hollow echoes. Nor had she gone more than a block before she heard an odd sound behind her.

Nella glanced over her shoulder but could see nothing but the swirl of fog. "Widgeon," she told herself stoutly. "There is nobody there."

She started forward again and had not taken a half dozen steps when she heard the sound again. This time she identified the scrape of shoe leather on damp stones.

Someone was following her. Nella's heart began to pound, and she felt chilled with apprehension. She now remembered what Lord Moore had said about London being a den of crime. She half stopped and turned back, but then realized that this course would lead her directly into the arms of her pursuer. It was best to keep walking until she met someone who could help her.

She quickened her steps. The follower did also, and a thick voice snarled, "You, there. Stop."

Nella bit back a scream as a man suddenly loomed out of the fog in front of her. "Didn't yer 'ear what 'e said?" he demanded. " 'And us yer rolls of soft."

She could not see his face, but his breath stank of liquor. Fear chilled angry. "I have no money," she replied. "Get out of my way."

"Shut your bone box," the man snarled. "Do as I say, or I'll slit yer throat."

Something snapped in Nella's mind. Instead of fear, she felt anger. It was the same anger that had made her lash out at Purvis. "How dare you?" she cried.

Wielding her umbrella like a rapier, she started forward. But before she could take more than a few steps, muscular arms twined around her waist from behind. "No ye don't," a rough voice exclaimed.

Nella kicked backward with all her strength. Her foot connected, and her attacker yelled and loosened his hold on her. She began to run past him, but her foot slipped on the stones, and she was caught and hauled back.

Nella started to scream, but the sound was forced back into her lungs as a hand covered her mouth. A blast of liquor-soured breath nearly suffocated her. "Search 'er, Bill," her captor ordered.

Nella felt a hand fumbling in her bosom. Fear made her feel faint, but disgust and outrage were stronger even than fear. She bit down on the hand that covered her mouth and, as the cursing robber released her, let out a piercing scream.

It died in her throat as a vicious hand caught her by the hair and yanked her head back, hard. "You'll be sorry for that, you!" a furious voice snarled. "Let's drag this 'ellcat into that alley an' 'ave some fun wi' er 'fore we cuts 'er throat. Wot say?"

"I say *no*," a deep voice replied.

Nella could have fainted with relief. It was Major Harcourt.

# Chapter Ten

"'O THE 'ELL—"

It was as far as the footpad got. There was the sound of a blow, and the bruising clutch on Nella's hair slackened.

As one of her attackers slumped to the ground, the other ran forward, but Harcourt was ready for him. There was a brief struggle, the *snick* of a bone breaking, and the thug's knife went spinning into the darkness. Seconds later, the ruffian fell howling and writhing beside his unconscious confederate.

Turning to Nella, Harcourt caught her by the shoulders. "Are you hurt?"

She tried to speak but could only shake her head mutely. She was grateful for the hard grip of his hands on her shoulders, for her legs had gone weak under her, and her heart was racing like a mad thing.

The thought that these slip-gibbets had threatened Nella had roused an almost mindless fury in Harcourt. Now that he knew she was unharmed, relief made him angry. "What possessed you to be so crack-brained as to go walking out alone after dark?"

he demanded. "This is London. There are men, and women, too, who'd murder you for a few coins."

She did not argue. "Those men. Are they—"

"They won't trouble you again," he replied grimly. "Listen, the watch is coming."

Perhaps the watch would have arrived in time to save her, but she did not think so. Nella felt nauseated as she recalled the rough hand fumbling at her breasts. She stood silent and still while Harcourt explained what had happened to the watch, and only when the dazed footpads had been dragged off to the watchhouse did she turn to the major.

"Thank you," she whispered. "If you had not been here—"

"Don't think about it," he said quickly. "It's over, and nothing has happened." Then, as Nella shivered violently he added, "Let me get you back to Colonel Karmer's house."

He put a firm arm around her shoulders. She did not object but leaned into the warmth and security of that clasp, and it took her several moments to realize what he had said.

"How did you know that I was staying with Colonel Karmer?" she wondered.

The familiar, dry amusement returned to Harcourt's voice. "In London, any kind of gossip has wings. I met Deering at White's tonight, and he told me he had seen you and Lady Linden in the park."

"But I did not tell them our direction," she protested.

"Lord Francis was also at White's, and he spoke of

the black horse you mean to race at Newmarket."
When he felt her slender body tremble against his side, Harcourt felt renewed fear. He had almost come too late to protect her. In fact, he had almost not come at all.

When Deering had told him of his meeting with Lady Linden, Harcourt's instinct for self-preservation had reasserted itself. He had remembered his vow to forget the unconventional Miss Citronella Linden and calmly, sensibly decided that any further contact with Nella would be not only foolish but pointless.

Harcourt had left White's with Deering and several others en route to a late supper at the Piazza Coffee House. But at the last moment, something had made him change his mind. If he hadn't, God only knew what would have happened to Nella.

Nella had no idea what the major was thinking, but she sensed the tension in him. "I am sorry," she said in a low tone. "It was idiotish of me to walk out like that. But I was worried about Angel, and—"

"Hell and the devil," he exclaimed, "when will you learn to think of yourself?"

They both stopped walking. He turned to face her, and she caught a glimpse of his face. That small glimpse caused her to catch her breath.

Next moment she was in his arms, and he was kissing her with single-minded passion. As she returned those fiery kisses, Nella knew that all through the days of their separation, she had dreamed of being kissed by Major Harcourt. Nor had she forgotten one detail of their first kiss. His mouth

was as sweet, h[illegible] her were as st[illegible]
Nella no lo[illegible] r or any othe[illegible]
[illegible]eable [illegible] and safe and
[illegible]ted. Yet [illegible]eart beat so [illegible]
[illegible]t she co[illegible] h. Excitem[illegible]
[illegible]tentment [illegible]lended in[illegible]
[illegible] thought.
She was in l[illegible] Harcourt. She
[illegible] steadily [illegible] m since t[illegible]
when he [illegible] rt out of [illegible]
the road. [illegible] she had m[illegible]
[illegible]n. Like [illegible] *was.*
[illegible] nestled [illegible] and Harco[illegible]
[illegible]nced an [illegible]nsation. He w[illegible]
[illegible]ys been s[illegible] a callow you[illegible]
[illegible] of fierce [illegible]derness, and p[illegible]
[illegible]had in[illegible] as something
[illegible]y new to[illegible]as were almos[illegible]

[illegible] ut one thou[illegible]
[illegible] belatedly,
[illegible] had been [illegible]
[illegible]er life [illegible] and he had [illegible]
No wo[illegible]ion could [illegible]
[illegible] actions.
[illegible]ntage of [illegible]
[illegible] require[illegible]
[illegible] a go.
[illegible]e, stiff voi[illegible]
[illegible] "I should no[illegible]
[illegible] that."
[illegible]stead of [illegible]ocy, Nella w[illegible]

forward into his arms and put her arms about his waist.

If this was shameless behavior, she didn't care. The only thing that mattered was that her major's arms went around her, crushing her to him. She felt once more the warmth and safety and the glorious excitement that flowed like honey and wine through her veins.

This wonderous liquor seemed to rush to her head as she heard the major say almost desperately, "Nella, my dearest one—this won't do. Sweetheart—I mean, Miss Linden—you've had a severe shock. You don't know what you're doing."

"But I do."

She raised her face to his and Harcourt, looking down into that vivid face that had haunted his dreams, forgot a lifetime of experience and good sense. He began to kiss her again, with an intensity that turned the cool April night to sizzling heat.

"I love you," Harcourt confessed against her lips. "My God, *how* I love you."

"And I love you, Charles."

Neither of them was conscious of having spoken aloud, nor did they actually need words. Harcourt's heart, beating wildly against Nella's breast, was evidence of his feelings. Her trembling hands, clasped about his neck, spoke louder than any declaration. They clung so tightly together that they seemed to be melded into one.

"I tried," Harcourt explained huskily. "I did my best to forget you. I left Hampshire because of what I was beginning to feel toward you. But once I returned to London, I found I could not get you out of my mind."

She pressed her face against his broad chest. "I thought that you had joined your regiment and were fighting somewhere. I was terrified that you had been hurt."

"My regiment has not yet mustered, for which I now thank God," Harcourt told her passionately.

Slowly, they drew apart and looked at each other. Harcourt's mouth tugged into his old, wry smile, but his eyes were tender. "So," he said softly, "here we are, my very dear ally, on the brink of committing a mutual idiocy."

She did not pretend to misunderstand him. "It seems as though we are, Charles."

"You'll recall that we both agreed that marrying for love would not serve. We were going to dangle for rich spouses."

She sighed. "I am as poor as a churchmouse."

"And I am not a wealthy man. I cannot heap riches at your feet." Most tenderly, Harcourt smoothed back a curl that had fallen across Nella's cheek. "Even so I must tell you that if I were to continue to live apart from you, I would go mad."

"That would never do."

He kissed her again. Their mouths clung to each other in a near frenzy of desire. The fog around them closed them in until they seemed to be in a world of their own making.

Finally, lack of oxygen drove them apart. Then, leaning on each other, they smiled luminously upon each other. "Marry me," Harcourt urged.

Blissfully, Nella inclined her head. "Yes!"

"Sweetheart, I cannot offer you riches untold, but at least I can offer you a living. Besides which I intend to sell my commission."

His words tumbled Nella down from the pinnacle of bliss to which she had soared, and a fraction of her old common sense returned. Her Charles's living might not be enough to support a wife and family, but she could not possibly allow him to sell his commission. He enjoyed his life as a soldier. He had fought hard for what he had.

"Don't look so stricken," he was telling her gently. "Soldiering is not all I know. I am far from being the helpless gentleman my father was."

Mention of his father stiffened Nella's resolve. If her major sold the commission he valued, he might begin to resent her as his father had resented his mother. "I cannot allow you to do that," Nella said, and added reluctantly, "Besides, there are . . . debts."

The glow in his grey eyes remained undimmed. "Your father's gaming notes—I know all about them. You've shouldered the load alone too long, sweetheart. Now I'm here, and I can help."

He bent to kiss her hair and draw her close, and Nella's heart beat fast with mingled joy and apprehension. Of course he did not know how great Sir Tom's debts were, but perhaps there was no need that he ever know.

"Charles, let me tell you about Excalibur," she said.

Eagerly she sketched out her plans. "He is entered in a special handicap for three-year-olds who have not raced before," she explained. "We are sure that Excalibur will carry away the purse. If he wins, we will be clear of debts and there will be no need for you to sell your commission."

He waited until she had finished and then said, "Excalibur is a fine horse. But he'll be pitted against the best animals in England. Are you placing a private wager on him yourself?"

It was on the tip of Nella's tongue to tell Harcourt just how much was riding on Excalibur's back, but she checked herself. She could not let him know how much she had to lose. "We do not have much capital," she said evasively.

Harcourt misread the shadowed look in Nella's eyes. He thought that she was thinking of Purvis, who would also be at Newmarket. The major had made enough inquiries about the horse fancier to despise the man, but he did not underestimate Purvis's cunning.

Abruptly he asked, "When are you traveling to Newmarket?"

She told him, adding, "That is more than a week away. Charles, do you think—*could* we not wait until after the race to tell anyone about our engagement? I would like to keep it our secret until then."

She was smiling again, and the shadows in her eyes were gone. Harcourt's concern eased. In fact, for a man who had committed the incredible idiocy of falling in love with a penniless lady, he felt ridiculously happy.

He kissed her once again and said, "Let it be our secret, then. But I am coming with you to Newmarket, my sweetheart. Colonel Karmer may be the prince of good fellows, but I'll feel better if I'm with you."

"So will I," Nella replied.

Next day Harcourt came to call at the Karmers' and made himself so agreeable that Mrs. Karmer was charmed. Later she confided to the colonel that she had been mistaken in her original assessment of Major Harcourt. He was a lovely man and had obviously conceived a *tendre* for dear Nella.

"They smell like April and May," she smiled. "They are *trying* to hide it, but I am not such a wantwit as to miss the look he gave her. Such a look, Colonel. It made me feel *quite* sentimental."

The colonel was more hard headed. "Miss Nella's got no time to think of love," he said. "Eh? She's put everything she's got and more she's borrowed on that black horse, and never mind May and moonshine."

It was this fact that made Nella so anxious. Before this she had wanted desperately to clear herself of debts, but now her personal happiness was also at stake. She reassured herself that Excalibur could not possibly lose. Daily reports from Newmarket told her that his training was attracting large crowds and that excitement over the black stallion had even invaded the sacred precincts of the Jockey Club. Almost everyone who considered himself a sportsman had a wager on the outcome of Excalibur's maiden race.

This was good news, but there was also bad. As she told Harcourt when they had a moment alone together, Torfy and Ableman had seen Purvis. "He also has a horse entered in the race, Charles. Torfy says that it is an excellent roan." She paused, then added in a lower tone, "I am worried."

As if to reassure them both Harcourt put an arm around her waist. "I'll be there," he promised.

Watching the hard and resolute look in her major's eyes, Nella felt her apprehensions lessen somewhat. But when he went away and she was alone, her worries returned. Besides wanting Excalibur, Purvis carried a grudge against her for the thrashing she had given him and would go out of his way to do her a mischief.

On the eve of the race, she was so racked with nerves that the colonel became alarmed. "Can't let others see her quaking like a pudding," he told his wife. "Bless my soul, it won't do at all. Take her somewhere and let her shake off the blue devils. Eh? Take her shopping."

Accordingly, Mrs. Karmer swept Nella and Angelica off on a last moment's excursion to the Pantheon Bazaar. This outing occupied most of the afternoon, and when the ladies returned, the Karmers' butler announced that Major Harcourt had called in their absence.

Nella's drawn face lit up at once. "Where is he?"

But Harcourt, pleading pressing business, had already departed. He had, however, left a note for Nella. Angelica, watching her stepdaughter's face fall as she read the missive, exclaimed, "Dearest, what is it? What is wrong?"

"Major Harcourt writes that he cannot come with

us tomorrow," Nella sighed. "Urgent business has called him out of London. He writes that he will do his best to conclude it swiftly and meet us at Newmarket."

"Then that is what he will do," Mrs. Karmer soothed. "You will have the colonel with you as well as *dear* Angelica and myself. We will make do, Nella, so do not fret."

But though Nella did her best, she was hard put to keep up her spirits next day when they set out. Everyone was nervous. The colonel had become as silent as a tomb, Mrs. Karmer talked too much, and Angelica twisted her handkerchief in her hands until it was torn to shreds.

Nor did the weather cooperate. As the Karmers' carriage rattled along the Ichnielle Way, clouds heavy with rain gloomed over the heath. When raindrops began to splatter down on the carriage, Colonel Karmer roused himself to remark that if the rain kept up it would be a soft track.

"That does not matter," Nella said stoutly. "Excalibur can run on any track, fast or soft."

They all felt gloomy as they entered Cambridgeshire and approached Newmarket. The old sixth-century earthworks known as the Devil's Dyke had a sinister look to it, Nella thought, and the rain worsened.

But the weather did not seem to have a dampening effect on the throng of people who were streaming into Newmarket. As the Karmers came into town, their progress was hindered by curricles driven by young bloods, stately carriages with crests on their doors, landaus and phaetons and humbler traps. All were laden with sporting gentlemen, young and old, lords and ladies in their finery, London tulips in bandbox finery, and red-faced county squires. They were all making their way toward the inns.

The Royal George, when they reached it, was full to bursting. The tap room was full of roistering gentlemen, and Mrs. Karmer clicked her tongue at sight of a fop in a yellow padded jacket, canary-yellow pantaloons, and a bright blue neckcloth tied in such an intricate style that his face was hardly visible. He was talking horses in a high, affected voice.

"It's true," he was saying. "I hev never seen such a wondrous animal in all meh life. 'Pon 'rep, I'd give meh soul to own him."

"Nobody'd give you a haypenny for your soul, Monty," one of his companions tittered. "That black stallion's above your touch."

They were talking about Excalibur! Nella, who had been about to follow Mrs. Karmer and the others up the stairs to the suite of rooms bespoken for them, paused for a moment. As she did so, she heard a familiar voice drawl, "Yes, indeed. That brute's a fine piece of horseflesh."

Nella's gloved hand clenched down on the banister as she saw Purvis leaning against a wall. He was watching her, his black eyes both mocking and hostile.

"No doubt the owners of that black beast think it will win tomorrow," Purvis drawled, "but I doubt it."

Nella swept up the stairs, but her heart was

pounding. "Depend on it, that vile creature is planning something underhanded," she told the colonel. "He will try to do Excalibur a mischief. He has been suspected of playing such tricks before, but because he is so clever, he has never been found out."

A visit to the stables where Excalibur was quartered allayed her fears somewhat. The black stallion had never looked to be in better health. His hide fairly shone, and he whickered joyously when he saw her.

" 'E's in right plump currant, 'e is," Ableman assured her. "Don't you worry, Miss Nella. Hexcalibur's workouts 'ave been the talk o' Newmarket and hanyone what is hanybody 'as a wager on 'is back. This 'ere 'orse 'as got wings like that Pegasus. 'E'll soar over the rest o' those cattle."

"I saw Purvis at the Royal George," Nella began.

" 'E's been 'anging about, but so what? Torfy and me 'as been taking turns watchin' Hexcalibur. No one gets near 'im but us two." Ableman added scornfully, "That Purvis 'as got a 'orse running, name of Spotted Dancer. Good-looking brute but not a match for Hexcalibur."

Torfy whispered agreement. Then, as Ableman walked away to talk to one of the stable hands, he lowered his voice still further. "Miss Nella, happen tha has had word from Linden House?"

"Mrs. Brunce writes that Miss Rosemary is happy and busy with her work at Portwick Hall. Mrs. Brunce and Rosa wish us luck tomorrow."

"Ah." Torfy blushed as he added hopefully, "Happen there's a word for me, too?"

What the housekeeper had said was, "I hope that fool of a groom is doing his duty to you." Nella decided to employ poetic license. "Mrs. Brunce added that she knows you have been doing your best for Excalibur."

"So she *is* thinking about me." Torfy grinned.

Nella was amused. "Is it not time that you told Mrs. Brunce how you feel about her?"

Torfy became so red that even his sparse hair seemed to turn pink. He mumbled something about not rushing into things. "But," Nella pointed out, "you have been courting her—in a manner of speaking, that is—for over twenty years. I am persuaded that she would listen to you if you declared yourself."

Torfy picked up a currying brush and began to work on Excalibur. "Maybe—but happen she wouldn't like what I have to say. Eh, ma'am, if Ceridwen Brunce tells me to go about my business, it'd be the end of my hopes."

"Faint heart never won fair lady," Nella pointed out.

She gave herself the same advice as she walked out of the stable into the rainy afternoon, but it did not serve. Nella knew that she should feel more confident, but her anxiety would not lift.

Supper did not help. It came later than was seemly and was served by a harried wench who slopped the tepid soup and banged the cutlery. The beef was tough and badly cooked, the chicken pie was all crust and no substance, and the ale was flat. Between her own nerves and the bad food, Nella could hardly eat.

"I hope," she exclaimed, "that Ableman is having

a better dinner than this. Nobody could possibly race on such fare."

Downstairs, there was the sound of roistering as gentlemen talked horses and betting and put away tankards of rumfustian and milk punch before progressing to bottles of Stark Naked. There was singing and laughter and arguments that occasionally erupted into shouting matches.

Mrs. Karmer clicked her tongue. "*Such* goings on, and at a respectable inn. Depend upon it, I will put a *flea* in the landlord's ear."

"It can't be helped," Colonel Karmer said. "Bless my soul, Lavinia, it is the eve of a special handicap. Eh? There are fortunes that will be won and lost at the Rowley Mile tomorrow."

Pushing her plate away, Nella got to her feet and went to stand at the dark, rain-beaded window. She felt nervous and inadequate and alone, and she had never missed Harcourt as much. Charles, she wondered, where are you?

"What is it, dearest?" Angelica had also risen from the table and was standing behind her stepdaughter.

Nella attempted to smile. "I cannot shake off the blue devils," she confessed. "It is idiotish, I know, but I would like very much to see Excalibur again. I have half a mind to go to the stables, late as it is."

Mrs. Karmer was inclined to laugh at such foolishness, but the colonel stood up and reached for his cloak and his cane. "I'll accompany you, Miss Nella. I've been restless myself. Then we can both get a good night's sleep and be clear headed in the morning, eh?"

The merrymakers downstairs were still roistering as, bundled into her cloak, Nella followed the colonel down the stairs. "Race fever," the colonel explained as they drove the three miles to the stables where Excalibur was quartered. "Natural to be nervous, eh? I've felt this way many times on the eve of a great race."

"So have I," Nella agreed. "That last year when Sir Tom was blowing at a hot coal and making wagers that he could not possibly win, I was almost constantly sick with nerves. He hoped, you know, that Excalibur could win and make all right for him."

It was late and the stables were dark. As they walked in a young undergroom came running out and almost knocked down the colonel in his hurry. His dignity much impaired, the colonel followed Nella into the stable.

"I thought you said that Torfy or Ableman was always on watch," he grumbled. "Where are they, eh?"

There was no sign of either groom or jockey, and the nagging unease that had bothered Nella all day became near panic. She picked up her skirts and ran to Excalibur's stall, then nearly fainted with relief as the horse raised his head at her approach.

He was unharmed. All was well. Nella's hand shook as she stroked the black horse's neck.

"There, my beauty," she began, then stopped as

she heard an odd but somehow familiar noise. Looking down onto the floor of the stall, she saw a slight form lying spread-eagled on the straw.

"Ableman!" she gasped.

She fell to her knees beside the jockey just as the colonel came up. "Bless my soul," he exclaimed. "What's the matter with him, eh? Is he hurt?"

Ableman snored. It was a long, happy, bubbling snore, and the colonel swore in disgust. "The man's drunk."

"But there is no smell of spirits," Nella objected. Then, as Excalibur snorted and stamped restively she added, "Let us carry him outside the stall. Colonel, if you will take his arms, I will carry his legs."

As they were dragging Ableman out of Excalibur's stall, Torfy came hurrying in. He saw Ableman and turned cheesy pale.

"What's happened here, eh?" the colonel demanded.

"Nay, sir, I dunnot know. The last I saw of Ableman was when he took my place so I could rest for an hour or two. He was reet fine, then, eating his dinner." Torfy shook his head in befuddlement. "We'd agreed that I'd catch my rest for an hour or two then spend the night with the horse while he slept."

Another snore erupted from Ableman. The colonel looked down at him with loathing, but Nella asked, "Torfy, who brought Ableman's dinner?"

"I dunnot reetly know, Miss Nella. He sent one of the undergrooms for a pork pie and a pint of ale from the nearest inn." Torfy's eyes widened. "Eh, ma'am, tha don't think—"

"Drugged," the colonel grated.

Slowly, Nella rose to her feet. "Purvis is behind this. The stable boy who we saw just now must be in Purvis's pay. Perhaps he was the one who drugged Ableman."

The three looked at each other with stricken eyes. Then Torfy pulled himself together. "Let us get Ableman on his feet, sir," he said to the colonel. "We'll see if he can't walk it off."

They did their best. Nella brought cold water to douse Ableman's head. Torfy concocted a vile-smelling restorative and poured it down Ableman's throat. Through it all, the jockey continued to snore blissfully.

"He'll sleep the clock around," the colonel said despairingly. "He's out of the race and we are at point non plus."

But Nella would not concede defeat. "We must find another rider for Excalibur."

The colonel goggled at her. "Eh?" he exclaimed. "You are asking impossibilities, child—I mean, Miss Nella. It is the eve of the race. Every available jockey is already engaged to ride."

Nella clasped her hands together and wrung them in agony. "But if we cannot find another rider, we will lose everything." Her distracted thoughts flew to Harcourt, and to the determined look he had had in his eyes when he spoke of selling his commission. "It must not be," she cried. "I will knock on every door of the jockeys' quarters."

She had turned and was walking out of the stable when the colonel caught her arm. "Bless my soul, ma'am, that won't do. Not a fit place for a female, eh? Besides, we don't want news of this to leak out. It'd be all over Newmarket tomorrow. No—Torfy and I will make inquiries. Carefully."

Their inquiries were in vain. When even Nella had to admit that there was not one jockey in Newmarket who was free to ride Excalibur, the three took counsel. It was decided that Ableman be conveyed back to the inn so that the colonel's coachman and valet could continue to work on him. Meanwhile, Torfy was to set off on horseback and scour the countryside for a suitable rider.

"And if there's a likely lad to be had in all of England," Torfy swore, "I'll bring him here by the scruff of the neck."

As they watched the groom clatter off, Nella tried to feel optimistic, but the colonel pulled his mustache viciously.

"Even if he does find someone, it may not serve," he growled. "A horse in his maiden race is all nerves. Eh? An inexperienced or bad rider can both lose the race and ruin the horse."

Nella's feeble hopes plunged. She knew that the colonel was right. Even if a replacement for Ableman could be found, there would be no time to train the man. Nella thought of the hundred nuances of movement, the intuition and the mutual respect that made a successful team of horse and rider.

"You are saying that I must resign myself," she whispered. "You are saying that we have lost."

The colonel looked almost ready to cry. "I'm sorry, child. But we must face facts."

She had always been able to look bad news in the face. She had taken her fences cleanly and not looked back. Now, suddenly, Nella felt as though the earth had opened under her feet and that forces too strong for her to combat were sucking her down. Into that raging maelstrom of despair, she thought she heard Harcourt's voice.

Poverty, Harcourt had said, teaches an invaluable lesson. It makes a man rely on himself.

And suddenly, Nella knew what she must do. Ableman was not the only one who could ride Excalibur.

She had watched Ableman train the animal and had helped in that training. She had ridden Excalibur almost every day of his life. She was small enough, light enough, and she had the skill.

For a moment Nella felt hot with hope, but then ice-cold reaction set in. She had never raced before. She was a woman in what was entirely a man's world. If she were discovered, she would be disgraced and socially ruined. If she were discovered masquerading as a man, she would almost certainly be disqualified.

Nella had one fleeting thought of what Harcourt would think if he knew what she was about to do. She almost gave it up, then—but she thought of Purvis's smile and the evil joy in his eyes.

No, she thought.

She would rather die than hand Excalibur over to Purvis. If she were to go down to defeat, she would go down fighting.

Once again and with all her heart, Nella yearned

to have Harcourt near. Perhaps the major would have been able to come up with another plan, but he was far away and she had to do the best she could.

But supposing her best was not good enough? If she could not control Excalibur, there was real danger of losing her seat. She had seen that happen to an inexperienced rider whose horse had stumbled and gone down in front of the field. Nella shuddered violently as she thought of horses' hooves pounding her slight body into the mud.

Colonel Karmer had no idea what was going on in Nella's mind, but he saw how pale she had become. He briefly considered calling Purvis out and shooting him, but he knew that this would not help the situation.

He put a hand on her shoulder. "I will stand guard," he told her in what he hoped were the ringing tones with which he had once led his troops to battle. "I'll stay here all night, and if that Purvis comes to finish his dirty work, let the blackguard beware!" He shook his cane combatively and then added more gently, "Heart up, Miss Nella. Perhaps Torfy will find a jockey. Perhaps my coachman and groom will bring Ableman around. Eh? We must not give up hope."

"No," Nella said faintly. "We must not do that."

"Go back to the inn. Explain what has happened to Lady Linden and Mrs. Karmer." The colonel gave the slender shoulder he held a little, bracing shake. "Get some rest, Miss Nella, and let's see what the morning brings."

# Chapter Eleven

DAWN BROUGHT TORFY, exhausted and pale. Nella met him alone and listened silently as he whispered out a tale of futility.

"I'm fair flummoxed, Miss Nella. Eh, I looked everywhere I could, talked to everyone I know. There isn't a jockey as I would trust Excalibur to. So what's to be done?"

Nella had been awake all night preparing herself for this moment. Now, she sounded almost calm as she instructed, "We will all say that you found a young jockey who can ride Excalibur."

"Nay, but I didn't—" Torfy stopped short and narrowed his eyes. "Tha'rt never going to ride him, Miss Nella."

"What choice do we have?" Nella's voice had a steely ring that silenced the groom. In a softer tone she added, "It is the only way, Torfy."

The groom was so agitated that he actually shouted, "But *how* will tha do it, Miss Nella? That colonel will think summat is wrong, and I'm in a fair sweat when I think of tha mingling with them other jockeys. Eh, they'll find tha out, and then there'll be disgrace with disqualification and hell itself to pay."

"Nobody is going to find out," Nella soothed. "We have brought Ableman's silks and his cap with us, and I will change into them before I go to the stables. Colonel Karmer will inform the authorities that there has been a change due to illness and that—that Ned Smith will ride [illegible] in his maiden race."

Torfy flung his cap down on the floor. "God damn that Purvis anyhow," he [illegible].

"Amen. Now let us go [illegible] the colonel that all is well."

Colonel Karmer was [illegible] anxiety [illegible] lack of sleep. Relieved [illegible] at the [illegible] that a jockey had been fo[illegible] to meet [illegible] Smith immediately, but N[illegible] off. The new man needed time to rest a[illegible]aint himself wi[illegible] Excalibur, she said.

"[illegible]nwhile," she a[illegible] to arouse Ab[illegible] one last time."

L[illegible]ng Torfy on gua[illegible] to the [illegible], wh[illegible] the colonel's servants [illegible] unsuccessfully to arouse Ableman. The [illegible] would not respond. Nella then took [illegible] silks for the su[illegible]d new jockey, an[illegible] off to form[illegible] the substitution [illegible] for Ableman.

[illegible] Karmer and Ange[illegible]. They, [illegible], ha[illegible]nt an anxious [illegible] rel[illegible] to hear that a [illegible].

"[illegible] will he ride as well as Ableman?" Angelica a[illegible] anxiously.

"[illegible] we will not [illegible]," Mrs.

Karmer put in. "However, I am sure that we will all be better for a good breakfast."

"I do not want breakfast," Nella said. "I am feeling a trifle down pin."

She looked feverish with her green eyes burning in her white face, and Mrs. Karmer worriedly suggested that she lie down.

"And I will sit with you," Angelica volunteered. "I am not hungry, either."

Nella had not foreseen this complication. She could and did refuse her abigail's services, but nothing would induce Angelica to leave her stepdaughter's side. Finally, Nella was forced to tell her the truth.

The words were scarcely out before Angelica uttered a muffled shriek. "R-ride Excalibur yourself?" she gasped. "You cannot—you must not! Dearest, you will be hurt!"

"Hush—ssh, Angel, or you'll have Mrs. Karmer in here," Nella pleaded. "I promise you that I will not be hurt. I have helped to train Excalibur and have ridden him since he was a colt."

She caught her stepmother's trembling shoulders and gave her a shake. "Angel, pull yourself together. You must help me."

Angelica looked incapable of helping anyone. Her eyes were glazed with the horror of what she had just heard.

"You must tell Mrs. Karmer that I am resting," Nella continued inexorably. "Tell her you will stay with me while she and the colonel go on to the races. Then you can help me into Ableman's silks."

Angelica was beyond horror. "You are going to put on a jockey's silks? But that would put you beyond the pale!"

"Everyone must think I am Ned Smith. Now, hurry, Angel—we must get rid of Mrs. Karmer before she realizes that something is amiss. And you must not let our abigail anywhere near this room, either."

Tottering out of the room, Angelica somehow convinced Mrs. Karmer that she and the colonel should leave Nella and go to the race. Then, she hurried back to the room she shared with her stepdaughter and stood by helplessly as Nella donned the tight green and blue silks.

"Oh, Nella," she moaned, "you look almost as though you are unclothed."

Nella had been thinking the same thing, but she replied staunchly, "Ableman has won a great many races wearing these silks. They will bring me luck."

Nella piled her long hair on the top of her head, pulled the jockey's cap over her curls and secured it tightly. "There. Tell me if I do not at least resemble 'Ned Smith.' "

The glass told her so. Looking back under the close-fitting cap was a face that could have belonged to a very handsome, if feminine, young man. Nella pushed goggles over her green eyes, and the disguise was complete. Then, she held out her arms. "Oh, Angel, wish me luck."

Angelica hugged her stepdaughter fiercely. "Good fortune, dearest," she quavered. "Do not fear, I will stay here and make sure nobody knows where you are. But be careful, I beg you. Do not take unnecessary risks."

"I will try," Nella said. Then her voice became grim. "But I *must* win."

The day had turned overcast and a raw wind, more suitable to early March than mid-April, was tormenting the Rowley Mile. Heedless of the weather, a multitude of spectators had crammed themselves into position so as to enjoy the first event of the day. Since this event was to be a special handicap, a maiden race for two- and three-year-old horses of any sex or breed, surprises were possible, and consequently the betting was high.

Blood horses with proud lineages but of unproved worth were competing against unknown breeds. Geldings, mares, and stallions, all approved and handicapped by the officials of the Jockey Club, were designated starters. Complacent or nervous owners, breeders, and fanciers of horseflesh were all on the lookout for likely additions to their stables. Gamblers of every description, gender, wealth, and class kept their eyes glued on the starting gate. In a few moments the race would begin and fortunes would change hands.

Leaning forward in the seats that he had reserved for his party, Colonel Karmer tweaked his mustache nervously and also stared toward the gate. "I feel uneasy about this, Lavinia," he mumbled. "I should have insisted on meeting this Ned Smith."

"But," Mrs. Karmer pointed out, "Torfy approved of him, and Nella seems to have confidence in him.

What *I* am uneasy about is Nella herself. The putrid throat is *rife* these days. Colonel, I think I should return to the inn and see how she is."

"Putrid throat be hanged," the colonel snorted. "It's nerves, Lavinia! Anyone who has staked so much on a horse as Miss Nella has done is bound to have loose bowels." He gave his mustache another tug, adding, "I don't trust that Purvis, His Spotted Dancer's running in this race, and—bless my soul, there's Harcourt."

The colonel shouted and waved, and a tall, broad-shouldered gentleman looked up. A few seconds later, Major Harcourt strode up to the colonel's box.

He was dressed in traveling cloak and mud-splashed boots that bespoke hours in the saddle. Even so, there was a happy, anticipatory look in his gray eyes as he bowed over Mrs. Karmer's hand. "Servant, ma'am. Colonel, I'm sorry not to have joined you last night, but a storm on the Scottish border delayed me."

While he was speaking, he was looking about him. With real sympathy, Mrs. Karmer said, "I am sorry, Major Harcourt. *Dear* Nella was not feeling the thing and remained at the Royal George. Angelica stayed with her."

"Miss Linden ill?" Pleasure died from Harcourt's face and was replaced with anxiety. He turned as though to leave the box, but the colonel had caught his arm.

"My dear fellow, I'm glad you're here. We've had a devil of a time while you were in—Scotland, was it? First, Ableman—but, bless my soul, the horses have taken their positions at the gate. Excalibur's post position is three."

"What's this about Ableman?" Harcourt asked absently. He was thinking that little short of death could have kept Nella from attending this race, and he was hard-pressed not to knock the colonel out of the way and hurry to the Royal George. Throughout his unavoidable trip to Scotland, he had thought of her constantly and wished himself at her side.

But if he went to Nella now, he could not give her the news for which she must be desperately waiting. In fact, perhaps it was nervousness and anxiety that had made her fall ill in the first place.

Mrs. Karmer seemed to read his thoughts. "If Excalibur wins the race," she said, "*dear* Nella is sure to feel much better. Depend upon it, Major, it is nothing *serious*. She is just exhausted and distraught after all that happened yesterday."

Just then, the officials' signal began the race. The gate flew open, and the starters thundered out onto the track. One animal gave way on the wet course as it lunged forward. Another pulled to the left. Then, out of the remaining field burst two contenders—a powerful roan gelding and a coal-black stallion.

Unheard in the roar of the crowd, the senior judge was reading the race to the other judges. Colonel Karmer meanwhile was shouting, "Excalibur leads by a short head. Eh? Followed by Spotted Dancer—Purvis's horse. Oh, bless my soul, Excalibur's taking the lead by a full head."

He broke off his narrative to yell encouragements, and Harcourt frowned in sudden concentration. He had never met Ableman. Then why did the small, lithe figure on Excalibur's back seem so familiar?

"On, Excalibur!" Colonel Karmer exhorted. "On, sir. Bless my soul—bless my *soul*, but that fellow Smith can ride."

Harcourt started. "Smith! What happened to Ableman?"

"What? Oh, I started to tell you that we had the devil's own time," the colonel shouted in the major's ear. "Ableman was drugged. Purvis's doing, no doubt, but nothing can be proven. Eh? Luckily, Torfy found a fellow called Smith to ride Excalibur."

Harcourt stared very hard at the tiny green and blue figure as it swept past their box.

Impossible, he thought.

Grasping the colonel's arm, he yelled, "Do you know this fellow, Smith?" The colonel shook his head. "Do you tell me that Miss Linden allowed an unknown jockey to ride Excalibur?"

"*Forse majoo*, as the Frogs say. Eh? It was either that or scratch. Miss Nella met Smith, but I didn't."

For the first time in his life, Harcourt was at a complete loss. Short of running out onto the field, he had no way of stopping the race. He cursed himself for not having come in time to prevent Nella from taking this desperate action, but since he had not, he had no choice now but to let her madness take its course.

On the grass track below, Nella's thoughts were galloping with Excalibur. The numbing fear that had crawled through her when she had first arrived at the course had gone. Gone also was the uneasiness with which she had mingled with the sharp-eyed jockeys, including the hard-eyed little man who was to ride Purvis's Spotted Dancer.

"Straight ahead and damn the enemy," Nella had whispered to herself.

But as the spirited, nervous animals were escorted to the gate, Nella had begun to feel physically ill, and it was difficult to give Excalibur easy seat and quiet rein. Almost, she had turned craven. But at last the starters were in position, the gate had gone up, and the field surged forward. In the following storm of curses, pounding hooves, and shouts, Nella had forgotten to be afraid.

Now, she felt exhilarated as she rose high in the stirrups and felt Excalibur run like wind. As they went two furlongs out, he was half a length ahead of Purvis's Spotted Dancer. "We will do it," Nella cried exultantly. "We will win this race, my beauty. Put your great heart in it, my beautiful one."

She kept encouraging Excalibur as they came around the bend. The field was strung out behind them, but out of the corner of her eye, Nella saw Purvis's jockey apply whip and spur to Spotted Dancer.

Momentarily he managed to close the gap between them and edged very close. Nella instinctively gave way and Purvis's jockey moved even nearer, crowding Excalibur. "Get back!" Nella shouted. "Give way!"

Purvis's jockey turned his head, and Nella caught a momentary glimpse of eyes distorted by goggles and pale lips pulled back in a feral snarl. Then, moving with incredible speed, the man's whip lashed Excalibur's side.

In the stands, Harcourt saw the proud black stallion being crowded by another horse. "Whose roan is that?" he shouted at the colonel.

"Purvis's," was the grim answer. "Oh, bless my soul, what is Smith doing? The duffer's losing control."

Excalibur had never felt a vicious blow. Outraged and astonished, he threw up his head. Nella managed to control him, but by the time they were back in the race, she had lost her lead. Determinedly, she urged the black stallion forward.

Spotted Dancer was now leading by a head. As Excalibur attempted to pass the roan, Purvis's jockey veered to the side, deftly forcing Excalibur into the path of an oncoming horse.

As Nella fought to keep Excalibur away from a collision, she realized that Purvis had sent his jockey out to win by any means possible. Neither he nor his jockey cared if Excalibur was crippled or hurt in the process.

Ableman would have known what to do, but she did not. She had no experience with tricks that were played by unscrupulous jockeys. If she tried to win the race, she would put Excalibur at risk—but her only other choice was to drop back—and lose.

Nella thought of Linden House and Angelica and Rosemary. She thought of the happiness that she and Harcourt could have together. And then she thought of how she had watched Excalibur foaled.

Tears of fury and sorrow brimmed her eyes and

rolled down her cheeks. "I cannot risk your safety," she sobbed. "I cannot do that to you, my beauty."

From the colonel's box, Harcourt saw Excalibur give way to the roan. He did not even hear the almost universal grown that rose from those spectators who had wagered heavily on the black stallion. He only knew that Nella was allowing herself to lose the race and that only one thing would have made her give up her lead. "Fouled, by God," he exclaimed.

Colonel Karmer jerked upright. "Eh? Excalibur was fouled? I didn't see it—did you, Harcourt?"

Instead of answering, the major strode past the Karmers and began to push his way through the crowd. His one thought now was to get Nella away before she was discovered—and disgraced.

As Harcourt strode along, Nella continued her doomed race. Several horses had passed Excalibur, and the wonderful feeling of weightlessness and the rush of triumph she had felt earlier was gone. Even so, she did her best, urging the black stallion down the last stretch until at last all hope was gone. Purvis's roan horse swept through the finishing line followed by two other animals.

Excalibur had not even placed. Nella felt too stricken for tears. All she wanted now was to get away, but this was made impossible by the crowds that were milling about the winning horses.

"Well done, Spotted Dancer. Took the sails right out of that black beast, didn't you?"

At sound of the familiar drawl, Nella jerked up her head and saw Purvis standing some yards away from her. He was congratulating his jockey. Fury shook her, and she wanted to shout out accusations that would expose Purvis for the damnable cheat that he was. But before she could do so, her bridle was seized.

"Get down at once," she heard Harcourt say.

The sharp note in the major's voice pierced Nella's anger. Startled to see him here, now, she began to stammer an explanation, but stopped as she encountered eyes that were as hard as rain-washed stone. Torfy, lurking nearby like an unhappy shadow, mumbled, "He *knows*, Miss Nella. T'game's oop."

Her rage at Purvis ebbed away leaving her feeling crushed and miserable. Obediently, Nella slid from the saddle, and Harcourt cast his riding cloak over her shoulders.

"Keep yourself covered," he commanded. "I have arranged that a carriage take you back to the Royal George. Torfy will escort you."

"Charles," she began, but he was already leading Excalibur away. Torfy tugged at her arm.

"Miss Nella," he moaned, "come on before the whole world sees who tha art. It's over, whether or no. The race is lost."

"I was fouled, Torfy. Purvis's jockey tried to cripple Excalibur." But heedless of Nella's words, Torfy almost dragged her from the field. She looked back over her shoulder and saw that Harcourt and Excalibur were nowhere to be seen.

Nella's slender shoulders slumped in defeat. It was over as Torfy had said. Purvis had won.

Numbness settled upon her as she was driven back to the Royal George, where Angelica was waiting.

One look at Nella's face told how the day had gone. "Is the news very bad?" Angelica quavered.

"We are ruined," Nella said. She tossed the crumpled jockey's cap onto the bed, and threw Harcourt's cloak after it. "Purvis's jockey fouled us. He would have crippled Excalibur, and I had to let him win. We did not even place."

The dull, mechanical way in which Nella spoke tore at Angelica's heart. She tried to put her arms around her stepdaughter but, pulling away, Nella walked to the window.

"I am all right, Angel," she said.

Angelica had never before seen her stepdaughter look so crushed and beaten. Timidly she protested, "But if Purvis fouled you during the race—"

"His jockey has evidently had experience in cheating," Nella interrupted. "He was very clever, and no one remarked the foul."

Angelica began to cry quietly, but Nella's eyes were dry. She wondered what was happening at Rowley Mile. Perhaps Purvis had already taken Excalibur and was arranging to transport him back to his stables. Torfy would have to deal with that, and that would almost kill the groom, but perhaps Charles would help him.

Memory of the way Harcourt had looked at her pierced Nella's numbness and made her wince. True, his swift thinking had saved her from social disgrace, but she was beyond caring about such things. "What he must think of me," she muttered.

There was a stir in the inn's courtyard below as the Karmers' carriage came rattling up. It stopped, and the colonel hopped out, assisted his lady down, then began to march purposefully toward the inn.

The sound of footsteps on the stairs roused Angelica. "Nella," she hissed, "they will soon be here. You cannot be seen in that—that attire."

She whisked the major's cloak out of sight and, picking up her dressing gown, enveloped Nella with it. A moment later there was a knock, and the Karmers entered. "I see you have heard the news," the colonel began grimly.

"I hear that Purvis's horse has won." Nella was astonished that she sounded so calm.

"Not exactly," the colonel said. Fierce satisfaction filled his voice as he added, "The blackguard was disqualified."

Nella, who had turned to look out of the window again, swiveled sharply. "*What* did you say?"

"Harcourt had just joined us when the race began. He saw Purvis's jockey foul Excalibur on the track. Man has sharp eyes, for I myself saw nothing. After the race he took Purvis's jockey aside and got a confession from him."

Nella's knees had suddenly gone weak, and she sank down on the bed. "What—what confession?" Angelica breathed.

"That he fouled Excalibur, naturally." A martial glint lit the colonel's eyes. "Harcourt must have thrashed the jockey soundly, for the fellow was eager to talk. Naturally, the officials of the Jockey Club declared Purvis's roan disqualified. He'll not see a penny of the prize money."

Mrs. Karmer added, "And *all* the wagers he had

placed on the match have been declared null and void. If he is not *ruined*, he is near to it. It is justice."

But justice would not help the Lindens. As the Karmers and Angelica left the room, Nella forced herself to face the future. She had staked everything on the outcome of this one race, and now they had lost everything.

Debts would have to be paid, so Excalibur would have to be sold after all. Everything would have to be sold. As soon as they returned to Hampshire, Nella knew that she would have to make arrangements for the sale of Linden House and find a place for her family to live. And there was Charles Harcourt's offer of marriage—

Nella started violently as there was a knock on the door of the colonel's suite and a familiar, deep voice asked for Miss Linden. A moment later the abigail came in to announce, "Major Harcourt is here, ma'am, an' wishes to speak with you. Shall I say you're still feeling ill an' all?"

Nella had dreaded his coming. She did not know what to say to him. Nella began to say that she did not want to see the major but then checked herself. She would have to face Major Harcourt sometime.

The colonel was downstairs making plans to return to London, and Mrs. Karmer was lying down in the other room, so the sitting room of the little suite was empty. Nella walked into it and saw Harcourt standing with his booted heel resting on the bricks of the little hearth. She had come in noiselessly, but he looked up at once and met her eyes across the room.

The hiss of the fire seemed overloud to Nella, as did

the wind that rattled the window panes. But when she tried to read the expression in Harcourt's gray eyes, she could find nothing there but concern. There was no condemnation, no disgust, not even reproof. The dull ache in her heart became acute pain as he strode across the room to take her hands in his.

"You're very pale, sweetheart," he said. "Are you hurt?"

His voice was full of tenderness and love. Nella had thought that nothing could be worse than it already was, but now she knew she had been wrong.

"I should have been with you," Harcourt was saying. "I did the best I could, but I came too late to help you. At least Purvis won't profit."

"Colonel Karmer told me," she muttered.

Harcourt took her hands in his and frowned to find them icy. He wanted to draw Nella into his arms, but she looked so brittle that he was almost afraid that she would shatter if he touched her.

"Purvis is ruined," he told her. "No horse owned by him will ever be permitted to race again. After all, it's not the first time the Jockey Club has had complaints against him." Harcourt's lips tightened. "I also called him out."

The words shocked Nella out of her misery. "You must not! Charles, a creature like that would undoubtedly play foul. He will try to kill you by trickery—"

"He refused to meet me, so I was forced to knock him down," Harcourt interrupted. "I believe I broke his nose and his jaw. But he was too craven to accept my challenge even when I proceeded to thrash him."

Gently, he drew Nella close to him. "I've warned him that if he ever bothered you again for whatever reason, I'd kill him. He knows I mean it. You and Excalibur are safe from him, my darling."

Nella pulled away from him and cried, "Don't call me that!"

"Why not, since that is what you are?" She did not answer, and he ordered, "Nella, look at me."

Unwillingly she obeyed, and Harcourt continued, "I love you. We have gone over this ground before. I said that I would wait until after the race, but now, the race is over. Will you be my wife?"

"No," Nella whispered.

It was no longer a simple matter of her Charles selling his commission. He had no idea what she had gambled, what she had lost. The repayment of what she had wagered in a last attempt to stave off ruin would take a lifetime. If he married her, Harcourt would be beggered by her debts.

He was frowning. "What nonsense is this, Nella?"

She pulled her hands free of his and, with the desperation of a trapped animal, managed a haughty smile. "I have changed my mind," she said.

Harcourt's eyes had narrowed, but his voice was calm as he demanded, "What game are you playing?"

Nella gave an imitation of Lady Barbara Hinchin's scornful shrug. "Matrimony is not a *game*, Charles. I am sorry if you are disappointed, but I collect that it was you who first said that one must marry for money." She shrugged again as she added, "You see, while you have no money, Lord Moore has a great deal."

Harcourt could not believe what she was saying. "Are you telling me that *Moore* has offered for you?"

"Angel did not want him," Nella lied, "so I had to take matters into my own hands. Lord Moore came to London about the same time we did, and—and the day before we left for Newmarket, he offered for me."

Harcourt said harshly, "I don't believe you."

"Someone in the family must marry money so that we can be comfortable."

Her tone was hard with unshed tears. Somewhere inside her, Nella could almost feel herself breaking apart. If the major stayed much longer she could not sustain her masquerade, so she must finish this horrible scene as soon as she could.

"There is no use looking so cross," she told him. "I collect that we would have suited very well, but you see how it is. I am sure that you will agree and wish me happy."

Unable to face the blaze in his gray eyes, she turned and began to walk out of the room. She heard his swift step behind her and next moment he had caught her by the shoulders and spun her around. "Be damned to that."

Nella tried to cry out, but his mouth came down on hers and stopped all sound. And as the familiar warmth of his kiss invaded her limbs and her blood, all other thought ebbed away. Nella forgot Purvis, forgot Excalibur and the race and her reasons for refusing to marry Major Harcourt. Like someone who steps from winter snows into summer sunshine, she leaned into Harcourt's arms and surrendered to the mind-drugging wonder of his kiss.

For untold moments they stood locked together in an embrace that took them out of time, out of place. Finally Harcourt drew away and spoke in an exultant voice.

"You don't love that priss-mouthed want-wit, you love *me*. To hell with wealth and comfort, sweetheart. Marry me, and we'll stand together against the world."

Yes, she wanted to shout.

But before that joyous word could rise to her lips, she thought of Harcourt's parents who had loved each other before poverty crushed them. Looking up into her major's eyes, Nella knew that she would die if she ever saw loathing for her—or worse, indifference—reflected there.

With a strength of will she had not known she possessed, she put her hands up against Harcourt's hard chest and pushed herself away.

"I beg that you will not enact a Cheltenham tragedy," she told him coldly. "I have told you that I am going to marry Lord Moore. You of all people should understand my reasons."

Without another word, Harcourt turned and walked out of the room.

Nella listened to his footsteps receding down the stairs. She heard the inn door closing behind him. As still as stone, she waited to hear the sound of hoofbeats riding away from the inn. Then, finally, she allowed tears to fill her eyes.

Standing alone by the cheerful fire, Nella wept as though her heart would break.

# Chapter Twelve

"Now, Miss Linden," the bespectacled Mr. Rooby was saying, "here are the agreements of sale for the house and land. If you will sign them, the transaction will be complete."

Fitful morning sunshine streamed through the library windows as Nella dipped her pen in the old inkstand on Sir Tom's desk. The printed pages before her blurred for an instant, but her hand was steady as she put her name to the document that transferred Linden House to the Viscount Arann.

Nella had no idea who Viscount Arann was. All she knew was that he was a Scottish nobleman, eccentric by report and very rich. Since Arann's offers had exceeded all the others she had received, he now possessed everything that the Lindens had once owned.

Since Sir Tom had left his elder daughter as the executor of his estate, she was the one who had to sign the fateful papers. At least, Nella consoled herself, Purvis was not going to profit from the Lindens' misfortunes. With his creditors nipping at his heels, he had fled to the Continent.

Rosemary and Angelica rejoiced over Purvis's downfall, but Nella only felt numb. In the past few weeks she had lived through every shade and gradation of despair, and she now felt merely empty.

"Are there any other papers I must sign?" she asked the viscount's solicitor.

"Only one, ma'am. The bill of sale for the stallion, Excalibur."

A shaft of pain penetrated Nella's numbness. The hand that held the pen trembled. She wiped her pen point, steadied her voice, and said, "I hope that the viscount is knowledgeable about horses. Excalibur is a prince among his kind."

Mr. Rooby sucked his teeth. "I understand that he did not place in his maiden race."

Silently, Nella signed the bill of sale.

"His lordship has many horses at Arann," the solicitor continued. "No doubt he will find some use for his black stallion."

Nella blinked hard to dispel the mist that had settled about her eyes. She hoped that the viscount would not gamble Excalibur away or sell him. She prayed that he would see the value of *his* black stallion.

Mr. Rooby took the bill of sale from Nella and placed it on a stack on the desk. His dry voice was not unkindly as he announced, "His lordship wishes me to assure you that you will not be, ah, pressured to leave. You and your family may occupy his house until you have made arrangements."

*His* house.

"That is kind of him." Nella tried to sound properly grateful. "When does the viscount intend to take possession of Linden House?"

"I am not sure," the viscount's solicitor admitted. "His lordship is currently busy with the ordering of his Scottish estates. His instructions were merely that all legal matters be concluded as soon as possible."

Now these legalities were at an end, and life would change. Unhappy but resigned, Angelica had written to her married sister. Mrs. Boyner was a disagreeable woman with a tongue like a wasp, and poor Angel would no doubt be treated as the poorest of relations, but there was no help for it. Nella clung to the hope that if she could find a post as a teacher or governess and if Rosa could give drawing lessons, perhaps Angel might join them one day.

Stubbs creaked up to show the viscount's solicitor out, and Nella's heart almost faltered. Now that the legal conveyances had been signed, she must face the next step in the dissolution of Linden House.

Forcing herself to sound cheerful, she said, "After you see Mr. Rooby out, Stubbs, will you and Mrs. Brunce and Torfy come and see me here?"

It would not be easy dismissing people who were as dear to her as her own flesh and blood, but all would be well. Ableman, shaken and angry but restored to health, had had no trouble finding work, and Torfy would no doubt be deluged with offers. Armed with glowing recommendations, Mrs. Brunce would find a decent situation. Stubbs, who had grown old in the house he had served for three generations, would go and live with his married son.

Nella sat silently in Sir Tom's chair until the servants filed into the room. Then, she spoke in a matter-of-fact voice. "I thought it only fair to tell you that Linden House, together with the grounds it sits on and all it contains, now belongs to the Viscount Arann."

"An' Excalibur," Torfy added in his die-away whisper.

"Excalibur, too. We must be sensible about this," Nella said. "The viscount is being kind in allowing us to live here until we make other arrangements. Lady Linden will soon go to live with her sister. As soon as I find work, Rosa and I will also leave." She took a painful breath and forced it out. "I wish we—we could take you with us, but we cannot."

Stubbs cleared his throat to quaver, "If I may make so bold, ma'am, I for one will be glad to forego my wages."

"We must be s-sensible about this," Nella repeated. "The truth is that we cannot even afford to feed you." Quickly, she continued, "You know what you mean to the family. We have been—been like comrades in arms. I wish I could settle a grand pension on you, for that is no more than you deserve."

She drew a small box that was sitting on Sir Tom's desk. In it were a pair of silver cuff links and a silver belt buckle that had belonged to Sir Tom, and an onyx brooch that had been Lady Elizabeth's.

"Lady Linden and Rosa and I want you to have these," Nella said.

Mrs. Brunce's face puckered up, and she began to cry. It was as though the Rock of Gibraltar had suddenly disintegrated. Nella felt tears brim her own eyes as she begged, "Mrs. Brunce, do not cry. Bruncie, *please*. There is nothing else we can do."

"Oh, yes, there is!" Torfy shouted.

Very red in the face, he confronted the weeping housekeeper. "Stop those tears, woman, and answer me. Ceridwen, wilt tha marry me, lass?"

Stubbs looked shocked. Nella stared. Mrs. Brunce shrieked, "Ah, dammo, the man's gone mad!"

"I'm not daft," Torfy retorted indignantly. "What I'm saying is what I've wanted to say for years, sithee, except I was too much of a clodhead to say it. I have my savings through the years. So dost tha. Between us, there's enough brass for us and Stubbs here to find a place. And there we can go on looking after the young leddies."

For once, Mrs. Brunce was bereft of speech. She could only stare at Torfy with eyes as round as saucers. Nella stammered, "That is s-so kind, Torfy, but we are not your responsibility."

"Happen tha art, Miss Nella," the groom retorted. "I have been with the family for nigh on thirty-five year. I have watched thee and Miss Rosa grow up, and I have watched thee tak' on more than tha can handle. Eh, Miss Nella, tha'rt a gradely lass, and the thought of tha going for a governess is something I won't stomach, and so I tell thee."

Stubbs coughed behind his rheumatic hand. "If I may make so bold, ma'am, I agree with Torfy. You and Miss Rosa must not be so far reduced as to go into service. And the idea of her ladyship living on her sister's charity is equally repugnant."

"T'gaffer's right," Torfy cried. "The family should stay together and pool our resources." He turned to the blushing Mrs. Brunce. "Wilt become Mrs. Torfy, Ceridwen, and make me a happy man? Nay, lass, I've loved thee all these years."

"Get along with you, boy," Mrs. Brunce replied almost coyly. "This isn't the time and place for talk like that." Then she added firmly, "But you're talking sense, indeed to God. If we all stand together, we can *stay* together. And so we will!"

Torfy beamed. "Then tha'll marry me," he was beginning when there was a thunderous knocking on the door.

Mrs. Brunce gave a banshee shriek. "Ah, dammo, it's that Viscount Arann come to throw us out onto the street."

Followed by Torfy, Nella, and Stubbs, she ran from the study out into the hall. As they started down the stairs, Angelica came out of her room to ask fearfully, "What is the matter?"

No one answered her, for Mrs. Brunce had thrown open the front door and had come face to face with Lady Portwick.

"Miss Linden," that lady boomed, "do not attempt to lie to me. Where are they?"

Lady Portwick was quivering with such agitation that the plumes on her bonnet trembled. Her form, squeezed into a brick-red dress with armazine skirts, heaved with agitation. She exuded such waves of hostility that Nella felt almost physically assaulted.

"Where is who?" she stammered.

"Do not peel eggs with me, my girl. I mean your

sister, of course," Lady Portwick shouted. "That brass-faced hoyden has eloped with Lionel."

"But that is impossible," Nella exclaimed. "Rosa is here in her room. Stubbs, please ask her to come down at once."

Lady Portwick's lips curled back from her teeth. "I would expect you to shield her. You Lindens are all wild to a fault."

Mrs. Brunce bristled. Torfy scowled. Nella said coldly, "You forget yourself, ma'am. I tell you that Rosa is here—"

She broke off as Stubbs came shambling down the stairs. One look at his distressed face gave her the lie, and Lady Portwick fairly shook with fury. "It is as I feared. That creature has forced Lionel to elope with her. They are even now making for the border."

Angelica gave a little moan and collapsed back into Mrs. Brunce's arms. Nella felt like collapsing herself but managed to ask, "What proof do you have of this idiotish idea?"

"This!"

Lady Portwick shoved a piece of crumpled paper under Nella's nose. On the paper were written words in a looping, boyish script, which Nella read aloud. " 'Rosa—I can't bear it any longer. Mama will never agree to it, so we'll go off together as planned and hang the consequences. Ever yours, L.' "

"*Ach y fy*, didn't I say so?" Mrs. Brunce keened. "I knew those two young people were doing more than mixing paints."

"Do be quiet, Bruncie," Nella snapped. "I cannot believe that Rosa would ever—"

"What you believe is of no consequence," the lady interrupted rudely. "This time you have all gone too far. If your father were alive, be sure that Portwick would have called him out."

A loud snore, wafting from the carriage at this point, gave proof of Lord Portwick's readiness to do battle for his family's honor.

"Lionel has not yet attained his majority," continued Lady Portwick. "Depend upon it, we would never allow our son to marry a hot-at-hand nobody like your sister. We will catch up to them and when we find them, Miss Rosemary Linden will realize what it means to besmirch the descendant of a saint!"

She sailed down the stairs, and Angelica wailed, "What are we to do?"

Nella tried to martial her scattered thoughts. "We must get to Rosa before that woman does, or she will be ruined. Saddle Excalibur quickly, Torfy."

As Torfy went off at a run, horses' hooves could be heard, and a curricle swept into the courtyard. To Nella's consternation, it was driven by Deering. Beside him, on Lancer, was Major Harcourt.

Deering stared hard at his sister's carriage and exclaimed, "Hoy, there, what's to do?"

Scowling dreadfully, Lady Portwick leaned out of her carriage. "What are you doing here, Deering?" she demanded. "No, never mind that. I will have you know that because of your misguided familiarity with these Lindens, your nephew has eloped with that brass-faced chit, Rosemary."

Deering burst into a great shout of laughter. "B'dad," he chortled, "never thought the halfling had so much in him. Goes to show, don't it, Court? Still waters run deep and all that."

"Stop chattering," his sister commanded. "Your horses are swifter than ours. If you are not lost to all family feeling, you will find your nephew before he and that creature reach the border."

She motioned to her coachman, who whipped up the horses. As her carriage rattled off, Harcourt said, "Your sister is right, Deering. Lady Linden," he added to the staring Angelica, "will you be good enough to go with Deering and show him the quickest direction to the main road? He does not know the countryside as well as you do, and time is of the essence."

Even at such a time, Nella noticed how flushed her stepmother had become. Stepping sternly between the advancing earl and Angelica, she snapped, "Torfy can go with you, sir."

"But this is a delicate situation, and servants should not be involved," Harcourt protested.

The young earl reeled around Nella and offered Angelica his arm. "Lady Linden, your most obedient. Will you come with me? Highly irregular, but Court's right—circumstances are irregular. Big dust up if m'sister finds those two young sapskulls before we do, give you m'word. Can't stand on ceremony at a time like this."

Talking rapidly, he swept Angelica away to his curricle. Nella was starting down the steps after them when Torfy came running out of the stable with Excalibur. "He's ready to go, Miss Nella," the groom cried.

"Excellent." Harcourt had dismounted and now turned to Nella to add, "You and I will go after the runaways on horseback, Miss Linden."

After their last meeting, Nella had never expected to set eyes on Charles Harcourt again. The fact that he was here, now, filled her with emotions she could not even begin to analyze. But there was Rosemary to consider.

As she hesitated, Mrs. Brunce rushed down the stairs. Thrusting Nella's bonnet into her hand, she tossed a riding coat about her shoulders. "Hurry, Miss Nella, my little one," she urged. "You can't let that fat old bitch by there get her old claws in Miss Rosa."

"Thank God for a woman of sense," Harcourt said. He caught Nella by the waist and fairly tossed her into the saddle. "Onward, Miss Linden."

Nella spurred forward. So did Harcourt. They rode until they were out of view of Linden House. Here Harcourt stopped her.

"We are not going that way," he said.

"But if we are to overtake Rosa and Lionel—"

"If you think that Lionel has any thought of eloping with your sister or anyone else," Harcourt interrupted, "you are a greater wet-goose than I think you are. Let the others comb the road. I have a notion we'll find our runaways sketching near Portwick Hall."

Nella frowned. She, too, could not believe that Rosemary and Lionel had any idea of running for the border. "Supposing that you are wrong?" she wondered.

Without answering, Harcourt urged Lancer toward Portwick Hall, and after a moment's hesitation, Nella followed. Soon they turned off from the main road and onto a path that wound into the trees.

"The lad has a favorite spot somewhere around here," Harcourt said. "I saw him one day, running from his mother's tongue. When I was a boy, I, too, had a secret place where I could find peace."

Nella was caught between hope that Harcourt was right and fear that he was wrong. The thought of what Lady Portwick would say and do to Rosemary made her go cold.

Suddenly, Harcourt stopped riding and pointed. "Softly, now, or you'll frighten our babes in the wood."

Rosemary and Lionel were sitting peacefully in a dell some hundred yards away. Rosemary was sketching a stream that gurgled down some picturesque, moss-covered stones, and Lionel was sketching Rosemary. Both of the young artists were so engrossed in what they were doing that they had no notion they were being observed.

Nella started to ride forward, but for the second time that morning, the major checked her.

"I did not come all this way to chaperon those brats. I came to talk to you."

There was a note in his voice that reminded Nella too vividly of that scene at the Royal George. "I have nothing to say to you, Major Harcourt."

Once again she urged Excalibur forward. This time, Harcourt reached forward and caught her reins.

"Take your hand from my bridle, sir." Nella tried to snap out the words haughtily, but the steady look in his gray eyes unnerved her. "Please let me go," she continued in a troubled voice. "I must go to my sister."

"After you hear me out."

His deep voice stirred feelings that Nella had thought were dead and buried. Almost desperately, she reminded herself that everything she owned including the horse she was riding belonged to the Viscount Arann.

She must go away at once without listening to the familiar magic of his voice—but Harcourt's hand on her bridle held her back. "Very well," she said in a resigned voice, "I am listening."

"First, there is the matter of Lady Linden and Deering. He is in love with her."

Forgetting her own distress, Nella cried, "Are not things bad enough without *that*? Deering will make her fall in love with him all over again and break her heart as he did before. Or—or else he will offer her a slip on the shoulder—"

"No," Harcourt interrupted, "he will not."

He tightened his hand on her bridle, and Excalibur took a step forward. Nella was now so close that he could reach out and draw her out of her saddle and into his arms, but Harcourt reminded himself of what had passed between them at the Royal George.

His tone was almost stern as he said, "I do not mean calf love. Upon his return to London, Deering finally saw Lady Hinchin for what she was. He realized then that Lady Linden was the only woman he loved."

It was almost a relief to be angry. "How can that be? Lady Portwick has called us people of little consequence and less worth. To her we are gazetted fortune hunters—"

She broke off in some confusion. Harcourt watched her flaming face for a moment and then asked idly, "How is your fiancé, Lord Moore? Has the happy day been set?"

She glared at him defiantly. "We are being married on . . . on August the twentieth."

Suddenly he smiled, and the hard look in his eyes disappeared. "Oh, Nella," he began.

Just then there were the sounds of shouts and the rattle of wheels. Looking over her shoulder, Nella saw Rumtum gamely pulling along the ancient barouche. Torfy and Mrs. Brunce were in the barouche, and Stubbs was crammed between them.

Torfy let out a crow of delight. "Nay, didn't I tell you?" he whispered. "I knew they'd be at that then favorite spot of Mr. Canton's that Miss Rosa told me about."

Alerted by this noise, Rosemary looked up. "Oh," she exclaimed in surprise, "what are you all doing here?"

"I might ask you the same question," Nella replied severely.

Lionel and Rosemary exchanged speaking glances. "It's Mama kicking up the dust, isn't it, Miss Linden?"

Before Nella could reply, Rosemary spoke hotly, "Why should Lady Portwick be angry? Why cannot we be allowed to sketch together? Lionel has been wanting to show me this place—it is divine and has the most wondrous light—but Lady Portwick would not let him take me. Finally, we decided to go without her consent."

She was interrupted by a halloo as the Portwicks' carriage barreled into view. "Oh, dammo," Mrs. Brunce wailed, "they must have seen us turn in by here."

Rosemary attempted a rallying tone. "Heart up, Lionel," she began. "Your mama cannot—that is to say," she added, faltering a little, "Nella and Major Harcourt are here, and *they* won't let anything horrid happen."

Harcourt dismounted and held up a hand to help Nella down. As she took his big hand, he smiled up into her eyes. "Courage," he said softly.

Setting aside her personal problems with the major for the moment, Nella took her stand beside him. In silence they all watched as the carriage halted, the footman leaped to lower the steps, and Lady Portwick descended.

For a moment she stood poised like an avenging angel. Then, dragging Lord Portwick after her, she swept forward. "So!" she hissed.

At this ominous word, Lionel almost dropped his sketchbook. "M-mama," he stammered, "let me explain."

"There is nothing to explain." Lady Portwick advanced majestically and would have descended into the dell had not Nella blocked her way.

"Pray think of what you are about to do," she implored.

"Step out of my way at once!" But Nella would not give ground.

"Lionel and Rosemary have done nothing wrong," she said. "They are friends. The note Lionel wrote was merely an invitation to go sketching together."

*"Honi soit qui mal y pense,"* Harcourt put in. "Evil be to he who evil thinks."

"Portwick," her ladyship ordered, "remove this woman from my path."

"You will need to remove me, too," Harcourt pointed out.

Lord Portwick immediately turned pale, fell back several steps, and implored his wife not to make a spectacle of herself. "Dashed boy's found, ain't it? He's not on his way to dashed Gretna Greene, is he?" he demanded. "Dash it all, Maria, let it alone."

His spouse turned a withering glance upon him. "You would say so. *You* do not have the blood of Saint Hugh the Brave in your veins."

"Oh, stubble it, Maria!"

In the excitement, no one had seen or heard Deering's curricle approach. Now, leaning over the ribbons, the earl continued to address his sister. "Portwick's right for once, you're making a cake of yourself. Perfectly natural for Lionel and Miss Rosa to be together, b'dad. They're—they're cousins. Nothing wrong in a man going sketching with his cousin."

"Have you turned Bedlamite?" Lady Portwick roared. "How *dare* you suggest that Lionel is related to this hoyden?"

Deering turned to take Angelica's hand. "Lady

Linden's just made me the happiest man in England. Consented to be m'wife."

As the earl raised the blushing Angelica's hand to his lips, Harcourt muttered to Nella, "I told you."

He was interrupted by a piercing shriek from the lady. "Wife? Deering, you are joking me. You cannot be seriously thinking of allying yourself to a family of gamesters and fortune hunters."

"B'dad, ma'am, guard your tongue." Deering's eyes flashed. In that moment, he actually resembled the portrait of his crusading ancestor.

As though none of this was going on, Harcourt now strolled forward to bow over Angelica's hand. "Lady Linden, I wish you happy. My friend does not deserve such good fortune." He then turned to Lady Portwick. "Naturally, ma'am, you are surprised."

Lady Portwick swelled like a toad. Before she could frame a suitable answer, Harcourt continued in a lower tone. "Don't be a fool. Consider for a moment that this Cheltenham tragedy is being enacted in front of servants and underlings. The lower classes *gossip*, ma'am."

Lady Portwick scowled about her and saw that her coachman and footman were indeed listening with pop-eyed interest. Torfy was grinning, as was Mrs. Brunce. Even Stubbs was showing his near-toothless gums in a wide smile.

"If you do not accept the situation, you will be the laughingstock of the county," Harcourt murmured. "Depend on it, my lady, they'll be laughing at you belowstairs all over Hampshire, and the gossip will soon reach London." Lady Portwick winced. "Not even a lady of your rank and stature could withstand such scandal. Far better to accept the situation."

Lady Portwick attempted to speak but could only make a sound between a gasp and a gobble. "What do you think, Portwick?" Harcourt continued.

His lordship came to life with a jerk. "Quite so," he bleated, "quite right. Wish you happy, Deering—and you, too, Lady Linden." He tugged at his wife's arm. "Dash it all, my wife wishes you happy, too."

"She'd better," Deering snarled, "or I'll never receive her again. Nor will any one of my friends, b'dad."

As the reality of what the earl was saying hit home, Lady Portwick seemed to shrivel and sag before their eyes. In an almost inaudible voice she muttered that she, too, wished her brother and Lady Linden happy. But as she was tottering away to her carriage, Harcourt checked her.

"A moment, ma'am. Lionel needs to apologize for worrying you. Next time you wish to invite Miss Rosa to go on an outing, brat, you'll take along a proper chaperon. Cousins you may soon be, but your mother is quite right when she says you must follow the forms."

Deering had begun to grin during this last speech, and Lady Portwick was hardly out of earshot before he exclaimed, "Well played, Arann!"

Even without looking at her, Harcourt felt Nella start. "Arann?" she repeated incredulously.

"B'dad that's right," Deering chortled. "You're looking at him, ma'am. Harcourt's old uncle popped off and left him his heir."

Nella could only stare, and Rosemary looked perplexed. "Major, can you be the rich Scottish lord who has bought up everything we own?"

"Yes, but it's a long story."

Harcourt looked meaningfully at Deering, who nodded and winked. "Get your drift, m'boy." He turned to the other assorted spectators, adding, "Come on, let's clear out. Miss Rosa, up you get with Lady Linden and me. Lionel, jump up on the back of that, er, thingummy that Torfy's driving, there's a good fellow. Then we'll be off."

"I must stay here with Nella—" Angelica began, but her new love silenced her by taking her hands and kissing them fervently.

"Believe me, m'angel, you don't want to do that. Besides, that ghastly scene with m'sister has left me feeling dry. Need sustenance, give you my word, and I don't mean tea, neither. Court'll look after Miss Nella."

Waving his arms, the earl swept the others along before him. Harcourt looked after him with amused approval. "I think Deering his missed his calling in life. He should have been a cattle drover."

Nella demanded, "Is it possible that you truly are the Viscount Arann?"

He took her hands and smiled down at her. "I am. Are you going to eat me?"

Pulling loose her hands, she cried, "But how can that be? Or is everything that you told me about yourself a lie?"

"I told you that my father was well connected. I never bothered to make myself known to any of my relations, since they shunned my mother." His lips quirked in the familiar, wry smile as he added, "My granduncle Arann was the worst of the lot. It's truly ironic that he should die without heirs and that I, as his next of kin, should inherit his title and estates."

Nella was speechless.

"His solicitors descended on me the day before you were to go to Newmarket and carried me off to Scotland. There was business that could not wait, or I would not have left you at such a time."

Nella felt dizzy. It was as if the world had suddenly emptied of air. When Harcourt had come to Newmarket, she thought, he had already been Arann.

"I intended to tell you everything at Newmarket," he was saying, "but before I could do so, you informed me that you'd had a change of heart and were going to marry Moore. Which, my love, was as bald-faced a lie as I've ever heard."

Nella bit her lower lip to keep it from trembling. "You do not understand."

She turned and began to walk away from him. It was not easy to do. Her knees felt as though they were made of gruel or some such unsuitable substance, and there was a hard weight in her chest that made it hard for her to breathe. From the sounds of footsteps beside her, she guessed that the major—no, the *viscount*—had fallen into step beside her.

"At first," he was saying, "I was furious. I believed everything you said. And then I learned how much you had wagered on Excalibur, and my brain began to work again." He paused. "I almost called Moore out, you know."

"You did not!"

"No, because I realized why you had lied to me, Nella."

It took all of her strength to withstand the way his deep voice caressed her name. "Pray do not address me so familiarly, my lord," she said. "Nothing has changed except that you are very rich."

"And you are very poor," he agreed. "I have bought everything you have, but a wife shares her husband's wealth. The exception is Excalibur, of course. *His* heart will always be yours exclusively. As mine is."

Once again Nella felt herself shaken. Even so she raised her chin and gave him glance for glance. "I cannot marry you, Charles. You must understand that there are enormous debts left unpaid. They would be a fine dowry indeed."

"If you don't marry me," he warned, "I will tell the world that you raced Excalibur at Newmarket."

"You would not!"

"No?"

Strong arms went around her. The next moment, Nella found herself being kissed. And instead of pushing him away, Nella put her arms around the Viscount Arann and kissed him back.

"It is blackmail," she whispered against his lips.

"Naturally." Arann kissed her again and added, "Don't worry about your father's debts, sweetheart. Arann's left me a fortune. And as for your dowry, you yourself are all the treasure I want."

Instead of convincing her, his words made her lean back in his arms and look up at him searchingly. His eyebrow rose in a quizzical tilt. "What is it that troubles you?"

"Charles, you once told me that you did not believe in marrying for love," Nella replied. "Can it be that you have changed your mind?"

The new viscount's smile made his hard face soften, and his gray eyes were tender. "What a pair of hard-headed realists we are, to be sure. You sent me away because you loved me too much to let me suffer your losses with you. As for me, I found out long ago that I can't live without you." He bent to kiss her lips, her eyes, the tip of her nose. "You behold a changed man, my Cinderella. With you in my arms, I actually do believe in the magic of love and romance."

With a deep sigh of contentment, Nella nestled closer to him. "Then it is as the old stories say. Perhaps we *can* all live happily ever after."